Folks of this ....

I was right in front of your face
They went right under your feet
You didn't see me,
but I passed by every single day

My guess is that you passed by them today
You walked on them yesterday
And you ate your picnic with them on Sunday

You've probably fed the same ducks
Jumped away from the same rats
And used the same bins

You've walked your dogs
in the footsteps we left behind
You've looked at the same views
Same waters, same woods,
same meadows, same wildlife
You were none the wiser

You didn't see me
You didn't know what I did
But you will now

When you lost control over your life
I gained control over mine
Whilst you paused your lives
and stayed inside
I wore out shoes walking this Town

Everything I did was in plain sight
But I was and am invisible,
I am a no one

By the time you read this I will be gone
But it's important that I tell you,
I'm confessing
'The Truth Shall Set You Free'

I'm telling you why I did what I did
I'm telling you where they are
and where they went
I have not detailed every action
nor composed a
Dismemberment for Dummies
The purpose here is to wipe the slate clean

But now that I know what's coming
My regret is that I didn't do it sooner
I would have had more time to live freely,
without control

There's no escape in the end,
not for you, not for me
But I do have a head start
I'm going to live my life on purpose whilst I can
I suggest you do the same

1

NARCISSIST ROAD

You might find

what's left of them

but you won't find me

Just remember

'curiosity killed the cat'

Leave them be
or
on your own head be it

1 Narcissist Road

My aim is to remain unknown, therefore this has not been proofread, edited or designed. Clearly I am not a professional, I'm not an expert in writing, as you will find; I'm just an expert in disposal and in being invisible.

There will be many errors in the writing but that is unavoidable as it is impossible to give this to anyone to proofread and edit.
I would be reported before I've had chance to tell the truth about what I did and why.

By telling it how it is and how it was and why, I am able to walk away with a clean slate and start again away from here.

I don't care if it could read better, that won't change what I did.
I can't fancy it up with words or make it more enjoyable reading; I wouldn't consider the content 'enjoyable' but that depends on what type of person you are, but there will be people that know exactly where I'm coming from.

You may consider yourself somewhat of a detective and think that you've worked out where they are, but to be honest that is relatively simple unless of course you are lacking in sight; but it won't matter to me, I will be gone.

But only a fool would go seeking, you would be traumatised for the rest of your life whilst letting loose the wrong, and worse, you will be betraying me.
My advice is leave them there, they are there for a reason.

I've done some stupid things in my life, but I'm not a stupid person. I'm lifting the load, I don't want to carry the weight into my new life.

This is my way of saying, this is what happened, this is why it happened, and where.
No, I don't hope they RIP they deserve purgatory for all eternity.

The drama in this house began way before I was born, many years ago as I myself am getting on a bit now. This latest string of events was way after the beginning, but just before the end.

Sometimes, but rarely, cruelty gets an alternative ending, an opportunity taken at the perfect moment, unplanned; in this case it will have closed the door on number 1 Narcissist Road for the final time.

Maybe it will eventually burn to the ground, taking with it all traces of every moment.

I live in a room, me and the dog, it is my house and fairly big, I've been here far too long. These walls have seen and heard many things, much of which is far too sick and twisted to be graphic.

I am no one, a forgotten, insignificant and fortunately invisible. I've done things, things that you would see as wrong and indeed the law would agree with you.

To be honest I don't see why these acts are wrong, we are constrained by the social structure of a given time; many years ago my actions would probably have been understood as fair play. What ever happened to 'an eye for an eye' ?
In the biblical sense it means the punishment should match the crime, however, if that's the case then it works both ways i guess. Considering my actions would be deemed a crime, I'm not sure I would want an eye for an eye on considering what I did.

I would consider being caught before I've had chance to live, to be unfair and unjust.
In reading what I'm about to tell you, I wonder if you would agree. I will never know, but you may gain some insight into yourself where you stand on agree, disagree, right, wrong.
It may show what type of person you are, no matter your upbringing, you have thoughts and feelings but i guess you would need to put yourself in my shoes; not everyone has that ability.

I did what I did for a multitude of reasons, like I've said, I don't feel that I acted wrongly, each act had its own merit, but what began spontaneously ended in premeditation. I had gotten away with the first, solved all the problems that initially came with it; I have to admit, I was proud of myself, proud to have accomplished something that was long overdue. Proud of how I dealt with the surprising results of the situation and proud of how I didn't panic and chuffed to bits that not one single being was any the wiser. I can't tell you the sense of achievement I felt. To begin with it was a bloody mess, literally, but I kept my head, unfortunately for him, he didn't.

As I've said, I live in a room in a fairly large house; I rented out the other rooms, this is how I got by after my situation changed, after everyone else had gone.

I don't know if you have ever rented out your unused rooms or indeed lived in rooms, maybe you can relate to the nightmare scenarios thrown up by some horrid individuals and maybe you are aware that there are some disgusting beasts walking this planet, if not I'm sure you can imagine.

The renting out of rooms was meant to be temporary, a means to an end; what happened in respect to that wasn't meant to happen. It was meant to be a way of financial gain and to obtain enough funds to get away from here, to finally escape, to live without looking over my shoulder; it was meant to be fairly simple. Rent out the unused rooms, save money, tie up loose ends, move on. But who would have imagined that this pandemic would have gone on so long and I wasn't expecting another lockdown.
The first was fabulous, it aided me immensely but this last one has inhibited; but you can assume that by the time you read this I will have gone, left before they begin to track our every move, before the digital ID is mandatory.

I was very selective in the responses to the room adverts, I knew exactly what type of person; basically I was counting on the sad lonely loser with low intellect or very private, quiet lonely loser, people who literally wanted a room with facilities and minded their own beeswax. No lounge, no socialising, no visitors; use of all facilities, go to your room, I don't want to know you.

My privacy is important, they rented cheap, large rooms with king size beds, everything was very clean. On the whole, in the end, the scheme worked out, it was just the beginning that didn't quite go to plan.

Considering my work history, how I failed to spot the signs and traits in that being I don't know. I shouldn't have been shocked when I found him out, but in all honesty I hadn't thought through why some individuals are private unattached lonely losers renting large rooms with unlimited internet with a very private unintrusive landlady. Wow he was trouble, like I said it wasn't meant to happen. It was most certainly not part of the grand plan, but he couldn't stay, neither could he go; so yes, I guess I premeditated.

However, this wasn't solely about me and my life, not like the previous two were, it wasn't literally about myself that time; but anyway, he went quietly with no fuss nor fight, never to be a predator again. I thought that beast was the last from within these walls, but that's not actually true is it.

Renting rooms gave rise to a monster in my mind, it evolved in my head from all the individuals that passed through here; it became a mashup of all their features, bad traits and offensive behaviours, a melting pot of misery. It shape shifted and morphed, mixing up their features, I didn't want to see it anymore, it was disturbing and made me think things that I didn't want to think. So I stopped renting rooms to snuff out the monster.

I'm not saying they were all bad, that would be an untruth, some just had bad habits, some never even used the kitchen, they literally used the bathroom and the room to sleep in. Nevertheless, they all had to go. These walls were already holding enough horrors of the night, spanning many years, it didn't need more.

My life is very private, it has to be, but I've always been private, I've had to be the whole of my life. But there's private and there's private; before I was private to conceal others behaviours, but now it's to conceal mine.
Privacy is now to the point where I literally talk to no one about anything much other than polite words in passing on a pavement. No one talks to me where I live, I've seen them come and go, I've seen the originals die off. Word around here is that I'm strange from a strange family, of that they are not wrong.
I keep myself to myself and my wits about me, a careless move may end it all before I've gone. I feel like time has stood still, with each passing day I feel it is another day wasted, it should be a day being lived in my new life, not still stuck in the old, in this house, in this depressing and doomed country.

I feel that I've gotten the revenge that was due in respect to one person but sadly it became too late in the day to even up with the all others, but don't be mistaken, there were vengeful acts. I did reap some satisfaction on occasions, like unplugging my fathers oxygen when he couldn't breath and pretending it was malfunctioning. I would dither and flaff just to see his lips turn blue and watch him gasp for just enough. But to be honest he revenged enough upon himself, he smoked so many cigarettes at least four packs a day, it got him in the end. He could no longer run to catch you or punch you

and kick you until you wished yourself dead. Surprisingly however, the mental hold was still there right up to the end.
Now that is strange no?

He became reliant on me but he was still as large physically and I was still scared of him; he has been gone many years now but I will tell you about him later. I'm not entirely sure whether my actions that evening had a hand in his admittance to hospital, nothing was ever said, no suspicion raised, but his machine was turned off ten days later.

But let me tell you, he fought that even; at 11am that morning despite having enough sedation to knock out a race horse (the nurse's words) he sat bolt upright and let out an almighty yell that rooted me to the spot, it was haunting. I can't even find the appropriate words to describe it, but those few seconds of a horror show imprinted on my brain for ever more; all these years on I can still see and hear that moment, his eyes huge and bulging, his mouth without his teeth wide open, the scream terrifying.

I hope the mental hold doesn't last my lifetime, did he know I wonder?
Or was it a last shout for help as they withdrew the oxygen and increased the sedation?
It was barbaric really wasn't it, as he basically suffocated to death in the confines of an ITU bed where they are meant to save your life, not snuff it out. But there we are, it all happened, all legally and with my mother's permission; revenge can take years to come to fruition, I guess she got hers.

My revenge was not planned either, the planning only came about after the fact, well it had to really didn't it. Though I did find that not to be easy at all initially, as they say, even the best thought out plans get kiboshed; incidentally the word kibosh is said to trace back to the french word Caboche (head) and / or Cabosh (to cut off a stag's head as a trophy) a fitting word in this case then.

The only plan I have now is to tell the truth and leave, pretty much at the same time, they need to be synchronised. At that point the rest of my life as an individual free person will begin, 'the truth shall set you free'. (John 8:32)

When the rug is pulled from under, when there is no one left, when you have no backup, no support and it is literally you, you have to dig deep for those survival skills. I believe it was then that I became an amalgamation of everyone that influenced my life deep enough to assimilate their traits. I used resources they gave me, instinctually and learned behaviour; I did what they would have done. I didn't consciously think what would so and so do, I just did it and recognised during and after that so and so would have done this. You would be surprised what resources you pull up when you have to find a way; you are capable of things that you've never dreamt of, the most unexpected, unimaginable is there within us, when needs must, morality goes out the window, boundaries evaporate, rules don't apply. Having said that, all rules in this house were bent anyway.

I am hoping that once these truths are out there and I am free, that in time I will forget all happenings associated with this house; that is hoped, but of course I realise that memories bounce back, like they are attached to a bungee rope they have a tendency to bounce back up. But once away from here and I've freed myself, maybe I can make new memories that will eventually replace those not wanted; new neuronal pathways made of good things. Maybe the 'mind pops' will cease, mind pops can be disturbing and disruptive, likened to mental hiccups, not quite like a flashback, mind pops are short and sharp. I'm referring to 'involuntary memory' the mental recall that occurs without effort; involuntary explicit memory (Proust) Proustian memory, sudden, unannounced memories, fragments of knowledge, images or melodies that drop suddenly and unexpectedly into consciousness, completely irrelevant to the moment in time to which they intrude, appearing to be completely random. They seem to come from nowhere, arbitrary intruders. I've lived over half my life, that's a lot of mind pops from way back to recent.

One particular recent pops up now and then, no relevance to anything I'm doing at the time, it isn't literally a playback, it's a nanosecond image of the hammer bouncing up into the air, like a bouncy ball springing up, that's it, the hammer boinging up into the air. I'm not sure but maybe this image reaccurrs because it was a shock, not a shock of the action as that was intentional, but a shock that it bounced off and out of my hand on impact, it literally sprung up in the air as though it had bounced on a trampoline. I was actually shocked at the hammer bouncing and doing little else. You cannot smash a head with a hammer, it's a lie in the movies, take no notice.

I am the last one living here but I'm not the last in line, there's one more left, out there somewhere, he hasn't been back for years. I'd like to think that in breaking free he has moved on, but I do wonder about those traits; what he experienced, the trauma, I wonder what he became.

All contact ceased many years ago, he changed his name too, I never tried to find him, he never returned. He blamed me for his life of hell and it is true, I couldn't argue that. Maybe he took his quantum leap and is leading a decent life. I hope that it ends with me and not him.

As said, they are all gone now, went in various ways but all dead nonetheless; my mother died that day with none of her offspring by her side, such is the mentality of those from within these walls.

They say you reap what you sow, but even that is untrue; I know perfectly good people that ended up with a raw deal and perfectly bad people who got away with blue murder.

I do however, believe in that saying 'no good deed goes unpunished', I don't do good deeds.

I learnt at a very young age that 'good deeds' can cause you harm, people can exploit a good person and abuse innocent kindness, which results in you having to keep secrets for the rest of their life, and potentially yours.

But let's face it, as we get out of childhood we then aren't just passive observers or recipients; we become conscious co-creators of our lives.

So why did it take me so long?

I didn't take the quantum leap into a new consciousness until I did what I did that day.

Only then did I take control for the first time in my life, and I am in control as I write, otherwise I wouldn't be writing this would I.

Taking control is not a revolutionary happening and the means I used to achieve this is as old as the human being's existence; but, I am telling you NOT to do as I have done; no hundredth monkey effect wanted, it is not acceptable behaviour and it should not under any circumstance be copied.

If your M-field is suffocating and soul destroying, then get up and leave, go and don't look back, don't leave it until you're backed into a corner like a rat.

Just in case you aren't familiar with the M-field that I speak of here, Morphogenetic Fields, a belief system, invisible organising patterns that act like energy templates prevailing in human consciousness. That of which I hold responsible for being the invisible force field surrounding 1 Narcissist Road. M-fields are your entangled life and your living reality, M-fields of limitation, stuck energies and patterns of behaviour that go on and on; the source of which were before you were born, that comes on through childhood, adulthood, the family group, the tribe. Emotional and physical traumas, painful and limiting patterns. The family system is higher, greater, older and we are unconsciously subjected to it, unless we take that quantum leap.

The M-field for this family, my family, is multigenerational that I am aware of, obviously it all began before those that I do know, and mine morphed with another, equally as bad if not worse when I married. I didn't see it at the time, why would I, he fitted right in, it felt familiar and 'normal'. Anything good wouldn't have fitted right in, it only took me 30 years to realise that.

WHERE TO BEGIN?

Where to begin here in order to explain why I am at where I am today?

All I can do is tell it how it was, and is, as simply as I can.

Why Narcissist Road?

It describes the place that I was born in and grew up in and about to escape from. (long overdue)

It describes the people I come from, was surrounded by and why I've become what I have today.

What is a Narcissist, Narcissism and are most people Narcissistic ?

It is believed that most people have Narcissistic traits, most but not all of us demonstrate Narcissistic tendencies and many people like having power and control. A quick search on the internet throws up varying information but the traits are common knowledge.

Exaggerated sense of self worth, excessive need for admiration and praise, exploitative relationships, lack of empathy, identity disturbance, attachment difficulty, emptiness and boredom, entitlement, exploits with the use of guilt or shame, demeans, belittles, bullies, intimidates; losing interest when they've won at the game, concerned how they look to others, a need to be highly thought of and think highly of themselves, arrogant, unempathetic, self absorbed, never think they are wrong, therefore never apologise; they need others to be self sacrificing, they are callous, aggressive, authoritarian, can be physically abusive and generally have a disdain for others, they will use and abuse for their gain.

Anyone of you will have at least one of the above traits and you will know varying people with several; does it mean we are all narcissists or is there a difference?
Many people with narcissistic traits are driven by the belief that they deserve the best in life, well isn't that what most people strive for?
It is said that there is a difference between a 'narcissist' and those displaying narcissistic behaviour as it appears almost anyone is capable of being narcissistic at least some of the time; a popular behaviour being 'passive-aggressive'.
The difference is the frequency, intensity and duration.

In this house it was constantly present, a wilfully, purposeful toxic environment where lies, exaggerations and false accusations would appear for no apparent reason but self gain, self reward or just to be nasty. Narcissists distort facts, make personal attacks, blame and coerce in order to achieve their ends. They expect and crave gratification, attention, validation; everything is a conquest and about winning. They instigate and manipulate, these are facts, I should know.
In order to gain psychological control, negative emotions are used to make others feel inadequate, they cannot maintain healthy relationships, be it work, friendship, or love.
They fail to understand why everyone else doesn't recognise how brilliant they are, how special they are; not like an average person on an ego trip as that passes.
The narcissist has a feeling of distinction and a constant need to have their greatness verified.

Imagine having to pat someone on the back everyday and let them know how much they are valued, it is exhausting, time consuming, draining and a complete and utter lie.

It is believed that children who were made to feel that they never measure up will go into adulthood with a fragile ego and become narcissistic in behaviour to prop up the inadequate self; but I think it takes more than that and what I'm talking about happening here, went way beyond someone with a fragile sense of self.
What went on here for four generations, that I witnessed, was sick, twisted, cruel and quite simply abuse. Secrets kept within the family, within these walls, like I've said, I hope it ends with me.

We were all wounded, the battle scars were secrets, not many outsiders questioned but there were a few; in all that time, only a few close shaves with the truth, warded off by a front. If those truths had of been investigated and action actually taken, would I be where I'm at today? No, of course not, I would never have met him for a start, therefore he would probably still be walking this earth wreaking havoc with someone's life and indeed I wouldn't have given birth to the spawn of satan, so that's irrelevant as it wouldn't have existed anyway. Taking them out of the equation, I wouldn't have the need to confess anything as the 'wrongs' I committed prior to doing what I did recently, were not as drastic.
I have considered that it was them that pushed me over the edge, but I have also questioned, is it possible that if not them it may have been somebody else anyway?
But I will never know, there's no sliding doors senorio here more's the pity.

So now you have some idea to what I am talking about, you may start to see why and how events came to be and why I'm not sorry for what I did and why disposal had to take place; how it became so easy I will explain a bit further on.

Obviously initially nothing was easy, I hadn't had experience in such matters, but it was all part of a subconscious plan that I wasn't conscious of at the time; as they say, your subconscious is smarter than you think.

It is surprising how the mind works in times of desperate moments, it races and what appears to be the strangest of things get thrown up; their relevance is only realised later on. For example, faced with his dead body on the floor, I remember thinking, involuntarily, "we cannot solve our problems with the same thinking we used to create them" and "the way we see the problem is the problem".

It took me a while to understand why my subconscious quoted them; simply not see it as a problem. If you actually ponder on that, it just becomes a matter of changing your conscious thinking. I was in a situation that required dealing with, it was only a problem if I deemed it so. I also remembered "do the best you can at that very moment with what you have", I most certainly did.

Everybody retains quotes do they not, but I have completely useless ones running around up there as well as useful ones; many obtained from years of study and annual training updates, to which most bear no relevance to real life whatsoever.

The other half of the quote to " do the best you can with what you have" is "then next time do better", of which I also did, with her. Somewhere way back I must have read some information that I hadn't really taken much notice of, it wasn't of much relevance at that bizarre moment in time, it was some waffle about aligning oneself with true north, that mind pop appeared to have no relevance, or did it?

As after I left that room I remembered a few of the 7 habits; none of which seemed to have anything to do with the current situation. What popped into my head was 'be proactive', 'begin with the end in mind' and 'sharpen the saw'.

I was actually intrigued, stopped pacing around and took time out to look up the remaining habits. I questioned that maybe my subconscious was trying to tell me something, some sort of sign. I'm pretty sure that a book written for business use never intended the 7 habits of highly effective people to be applied to such a situation as this; it may be appropriate here to apologize then, but I'm not going to as I'm not sorry. I didn't write it, he did, therefore it is his responsibility, he should have thought about the consequences of writing such things and to how it would be applied; besides, I don't like that name. However, I will acknowledge that the 7 habits are in fact pretty effective, so thanks for that, but I'm not a highly effective person, clearly.

In case you aren't familiar with the 7 habits, they are, in order: Be proactive, Begin with the end in mind, Put first things first, Think win win, Seek first to understand, then to be understood, Synergize, Sharpen the saw.

I was most certainly proactive, I ended decades of misery, closed his m-field and I had the last word and the last laugh.

Begin with the end in mind, yep, his end.

I actually did have to sharpen the saw, well several actually, several times.

I applied first things first, dealing with that immediate situation, the recently deceased on the kitchen floor, well not that recent to be honest as by the time I got my act together several hours had passed.

It was a bit messy and smelly, I didn't have plastic or anything that you see in the movies, I had no idea where to begin initially.

Can I just say, that old saying about dogs howling when their owners die, It's not true, they sniffed him and walked away, one went to the food bowl and had a munch even, they didn't seem at all perturbed; I did ensure their routine was kept, but anyway, sadly one passed away a few months later.
That was a terrible time, I was almost beside myself, poor little thing was already diseased but such a stoic creature I had been none the wiser; but looking back the signs were there, the lethargy, laying in holes in the garden, not eating as much, not wanting to go out as much and not as far. I put it down to age but it wasn't, I was incredibly sad to see her go, I still miss her even now.

Anyway, I have no idea how much he weighed, he did have a bit of a gut, but let me tell you, a dead weight is shockingly heavy. I'm not a particularly big person, it was idiocy to think that I could simply drag him up the stairs, by the time I had got to the kitchen doorway I was exhausted, plus I realised I was creating somewhat of a mess. I had forgotten that when people die, bodily fluids and the like, simply let go, the smell is actually nasty, worse with him I'm sure; always cooking up some concoction and stuffing his face, such the 'pig at a trough' that he was. Shovelling it in quick, his swallowing had this gulping sound, I had wondered over the years if he actually chewed any of it; food used to be in the corners of his mouth, he would talk whilst eating, these were his 'in house' behaviours. Outside behaviours were different; he changed his behaviours according to the act, multiple characters for multiple scenes, I'd seen them all over the years.

Well anyway, the 7 habits; put first things first, basically step by step, so you could say in priority order, that's how I dealt with it all from start to finish.

Think win win, to be honest I had already won, I had finally taken control, but each step of the way thereafter, that was completed successfully was a win; if at any stage I had of been caught in the act, I would have lost.

Although not until I have left here and began my new life will I truly have won.

Seek to understand then to be understood, well I didn't have to seek much to understand why I did what I did, nor why every person from within these walls were like they were; my hope is that after reading all this that I will be understood by you. In explaining as simply as I can and in going way back, that you will understand how the present came to be; so in short, my aim is to be understood.

Synergize, well I acted alone initially didn't I, but I did interact with and was cooperated with, in order to achieve a greater outcome than had I attempted so alone.

Positive teamwork, me and my dogs / dog, the land, the rats, the fox, the water, the wildlife, the ducks, the wastelands and the bin man who answered my question that day, when I asked him "where does the contents of the fly ridden dog poo bins go, hope not landfill" ?

"No, they go straight to the incinerator".

So ultimately the incinerator people cooperated, as did the developers in creating the floodlands, as did my dog's need for meat, so yes, synergy, which in this case is more like **sin-energy**.

Speaking of sin, consider the 7 deadly sins, surely they are only appropriate if one is religious, or should it be seen simply as a break from moral code, that of which applies to a given time and given culture, which of course varies.

What are the 7 deadly sins anyway? Pride, Greed, Lust, Envy, Gluttony, Wrath, Sloth.

What an absolute load of bull, designed by the church to keep you oppressed and them in control. Stark difference from the 7 habits designed to aid you to take control.

But as far as the 7 deadly sins go, I am only guilty of wrath, however, wrath in this context was simply justice, justice isn't a sin.

I may have been guilty of morose delectation, the dwelling with enjoyment on evil thoughts, of which I had many whilst planning particular disposals, the places had to be more than simply convenient and safe, they had to have a bit of a twist and have some meaning. Not all as that would have been just ridiculous and would have likened to a needle in a haystack, too many parts.

The first disposal I was wary of course, so that was literally down to safe and secure. Once that was achieved I knew I was good to go. Ironically I used a meat cleaver that had sat in a case with the butcher's set for several years, it had meaning and I enjoyed using it.

Many years ago he did some computer wiring set up task for a women he worked with, back and forth he used to go, he said he was being paid, but of course it was just one of his many lies. I knew exactly what was going on there, he did the task to look good whilst having fun and eventually he came back with this set saying she couldn't afford to pay him. The case went straight into the shed where it remained for several years, until I used it for him. It had meaning and I thought many things and thought about it after the fact too, ha, justice and morose delectation.

I still have the case and contents, I'm not sure what to do with it, it isn't biodegradable, you can't put it in a bin, it's too big, it will be found, can't be dumped, so I guess I will take it with me when I leave and dispose of it bit by bit once I'm out, once I've driven a thousand miles; separate it all here and there, it's too conspicuous. I thought about disposing of it separately in the waters round here but they are all heavy and sharp, if found it would be obvious why they were dumped; tricky, my instinct tells me no.

Not that they would be found considering the actual state of some of these areas around here, but they may one day drain the ditches, tidy the wastelands; maybe they never will and if they do it will be many years from now, I will probably be dead myself from old age by then. But they may find a way to drain the meadows and continue to build without the nearby houses flooding and in not losing the main road out of town. Maybe the land will never allow it, but they did find a way to build in that area in order to supply the pubs, but that sent the water elsewhere covering land permanently, that otherwise only periodically flooded.

Eventually paths that had been there for years ended up under water, impassable due to development. Where sheep once grazed all the time, is now frequented by ducks, herrings, geese, moorhens, seagulls and floating garbage, fly tipped junk and body parts of varying species. Some days it stinks, some days it sparkles in the sun, but in the evenings there are many moncjac and at night enough foxes and rats to consume decaying consumables.

They may eventually find a better use of all that land, I say better use, but aside from the discarded garbage, it serves the wildlife well; the day they drain it, the signs will come down 'warning.. Path liable to flooding'. After they've stripped it, dug it, piped it, they will find all manner of things, but i won't be here then.

I like it down there, it's a vast area, the wasteland transcended by small streams, rivers, bridges, overgrown brambles, fallen trees, pointless signs on sunken fences saying keep out; you'd need a boat to get in!

There's a rickety path, water either side, not always passable; either side of the waters is wasteland, overgrown and unloved. It's always dark down there, the trees are old as the hills, fallen, broken, creepy at night.

I passed the tree with the face and the green triangle, where it looks like the beer has spilled into the river. Brown, like swirling toffee, when settled it looks like fudge, disturbing it makes it swirl, swirling sludgy beer; what a fitting place for his big mouth and greedy beady eyes, may he be forced to swallow the rat infected, contaminated sludge beer for all eternity.

Just so you know, I stapled his eyelids open, I had seen that many years ago in an old movie where they buried some men standing up with just their heads above the sand. They sowed their eyelids open, all the ants came and ate their eyeballs, except they were alive, now that's barbaric, at least he was dead and detached, in more ways than one.

No, no I didn't just chuck it in the river, that would have been stupid, as although initially heads sink in the water, after several days decomposition generates gases in the cranium, meaning potentially his head would pop up in the water. Imagine the scare someone would get seeing a head bobbing about half eaten by vermin; that could cause someone to have a heart attack or fall into the sludge beer and possibly drown. As amusing as that image is, I wouldn't want to be responsible for another death nor do I wish to be caught, so, he has securely gone to hell, from whence he came; like I said, the area is unloved by humans, not by wildlife.

In all the times I've walked through there I've only seen a handful of people. The path doesn't allow you to pass, you have to stand on the edge in particular places to let someone pass by, but not during lockdown, I saw no one.

It rained and it rained, at times it was actually freezing for that time of year and I had the shakes; I'm not sure if that was the wet or the excitement. As time went on the weather improved thankfully, my left hand was lockdown, the right was the dog. After that particular disposal I passed by daily for a while to make sure, shining the torch to ensure I wasn't going to unintentionally play football; all I ever saw were the glistening eyes of the animals. It's been many months now, the hardest task was a success and everything was easier from there on in.

During lockdown the only people really out and about without good reason were us dog walkers, once, twice, three times a day; the evening one not many of anyone were about.

I made sure I walked past the police station every single day, some older women with a backpack walking her dog several miles every single night regardless of the weather. I had already searched for where the CCTV are in this town, there aren't actually that many but I began to realise that it didn't make any difference anyway as loads of houses and properties have CCTV and even doorbells do, so that knowledge was irrelevant.

I hid my acts in plain sight, most people don't see what they see every day; I was and am, invisible. No one takes any notice of an ageing women walking with a dog, purposely dressed in clothes that have seen better days and which had become a bit oversized; the puffy old coat with the very handy large pockets which covered the baggy tops and allowed for a big baggy jumper that gave a rounded appearance; no make up, no jewelry, hair tied back like an old school mistress, an old backpack and nothing else.

For over a year I have not had my hair cut or done, not carried a handbag or a purse, not worn particularly feminine clothes, not touched makeup; I have lived invisibly in plain sight.

Don't get me wrong, I'm clean, just perfectly slightly unkempt and dull. I don't strike up or engage in conversations, the aim has been to not draw attention, there literally is nothing to see here.

I have also discovered that slipping under the radar in this country is terribly easy, no one checks to see why you've not visited a gp or a dentist; there aren't enough dentists and most of the population aren't assigned one and the pandemic caused everything to close down, including gp surgeries.

Restriction, unavailable services, a bad time for most, a perfect time to disappear for some. If your email and phone number isn't attached to many agencies, during that time it was easy to become detached from most if not all systems.

If you pay your bills on time, keep your bank tidy and your house in order, people have no need to contact you. This pandemic has been my co-conspirator, my partner in crime, but I am aware that it has wrecked many people's lives and worse. It caused death and destruction, I only used that to my advantage.

There was one time a bloke with a dog kept talking, he was rambling on about various random things, I initially thought he had some nervous disposition, until he said "don't mind me, I talk shit, I have a brain tumor".

Due to the field of work I was in for many years, my 6th sense told me he wasn't bullshitting.

I entertained him for a while as I didn't perceive him as a threat, he was either going to forget our brief encounter or die, so it didn't matter. It was just before one of the disposals, he asked me what was in my backpack, was it drugs? I said no, body parts, he laughed, so did I, he carried on walking whilst I continued slowly up the worn grass path.

The path of which Mary-ann looks down on as you go through the iron gate. I always smile when I see that name, not due to any fondness as obviously I never knew her personally, she died many many years ago; the smile is because that is what a previous work superior used to call him, a mary-ann.

Her term was referring to having his head stuck up his backside and basically being useless. She was correct in respect to the context of that job that we were doing, he didn't pull his weight and he didn't listen. Mary-ann very much had a meaning as did the plaque on the wall nearby, pertaining to how a wife should be.

As I completed my disposal, I stood up and looked around and felt very calm and confident that I had chosen well. A sort of triangle where old religion meets new religion, where religion looks down to where current crime and old justice sit side by side. Right there under your feet, surrounded by many skull and crossbones where the sunflower stands out; to me it looks like a stone of sacrifice from a horror movie and you can turn around to literally scrape your boots.

The times that I have subsequently walked through here, taken a seat and watched people walk over him; I've often thought about that song 'fool on the hill', as I take it's meaning refers to the fool knowing what others do not.

In the winter evenings this is an odd place to be, a bit spooky but you can sit up the top and look across at the fields; some nights when it's clear it looks like the stars are dancing on them.

Speaking of stars, I had a good telescope some years back, it was amazing looking at Saturn's rings, but he got angry one day and threw it out the bedroom window, it smashed on the drive below. That was the end of that. I was upset about it but not as upset as a person should be, I had grown accustomed to my things being smashed, well not just mine actually.

Aside from the frequent occurrences of coffee cups being smashed on walls, wine glasses, plates of food, remote controls, mobile phones, he ripped his own clothes off (at this I am laughing as I write) yes, he used to rip clothes from himself in rages.

Shirt buttons would fly across the room, sleeves would be ripped from the shoulders and sometimes still be attached to him via the cuff around the wrist; you should have seen the added fit of rage due to his own hand being the obstruction to getting the sleeve off, what was this ridiculous behaviour.

Despite the atmosphere in the room being highly charged and tense, there was something comical in the scenes that unfolded, but he was mean nonetheless; better in that he was acting upon himself than when he acted upon others.

We hadn't been married that long when he smashed my prize possession. When I was growing up my grandmother on my mum's side (who also haunts these walls) partook in a Sunday paper round. This paper round came about via her step son (more on that later) who built up a business in newspapers around the town; to cut a long story short, he died (just as well) his wife (long suffering) sold off the rounds but my grandmother continued this particular round for the newsagent who bought it. Anyway, for several years I was allocated the chore of helping her, then in my teens my father bought the round and I had to learn about sale or return.

The papers were delivered to the house, stacks and stacks of the blooming things. I had to get up early every sunday morning, sort the papers and door number them; then go out and deliver them (a few hundred) using an old pram and return to refill. Once that was done I would then come back, have a drink, wash the print off, change clothes, get the money bag and ledger, make sure I had enough change, then go back out to collect the monies.

Some people would leave the money outside (you could in those days, there was a way of life back then called 'don't shit on your own doorstep') Some people would take two calls and some you knew you had to wait for church to be done; some people would yell "come in" and you had to endure their weekly catch up of gossip or family news to share, it was all part of the service and you respected your elders even if you were just not interested, which I wasn't.

Once all money was collected, counted, ledger updated, papers paid for, the profit was mine.

From this small profit I saved and saved to buy my own portable TV. I cannot tell you what it felt like that day, chuffed to bits is an understatement; maybe you can relate to buying your first long awaited item that you worked and saved for, the first object that you really really wanted of which you obtained all by your own means, fantastic no?

I could pick up TV in my tiny box room and my sunday afternoons were mine; I would hide in my room and watch all the programs that my dad termed garbage and were never allowed on in the lounge, the waltons, little house on the prairie, all creatures great and small, butterflies and the like, without much interruption.

I would escape for a few hours and just be me, away from anything that had evolved in the room below.

He purposefully picked up that TV and smashed it into smithereens down the stairs. I did cry, he smashed my sanctuary.

But over the years he smashed so much stuff that it became normality and I guess is the reason why I am not materialistic, they're just objects to which one should not form an attachment. Now that I'm not forever cleaning up his trail of destruction, I find myself wondering why I didn't smash him over the head years ago, but I guess, back then I didn't have the weighty Le Creuset 'Doufeu'. I am not entirely sure why I chose this weapon out of all the Le Creuset on that unit, maybe because it was yellow and I knew it weighed a ton.

Anyway, several years back just after dad died, I decided to get a better education and train in a particular area, so I paid for and went to college. In my non working, non domestic duties time, I studied. One evening I came home from work and he had made a bonfire on the garden path, I was warned on coming in the door that he was 'on one'. When I went to investigate, he had made a bonfire and set light to all my college books. He burnt the lot. Not only was that an expensive act, it was nasty and an obvious silent statement.

But I went and got them all again, you had to have them to do the course, I completed that course, passed all exams despite him throwing rages the nights before, I sat several exams with no sleep and swollen eyes.

Despite the environment, my stubbornness was stronger, good or bad I don't know, stupid maybe? Or that my smarter subconscious was attempting to educate itself in order to wake me up, to get me to leave, or in fact to get me to look in the mirror!

After that course I embarked on a career, changed jobs, went into a particular profession of which should be no surprise really, as they say, 'it takes one to recognise one'.

Anyway, I was then funded by that establishment to do a masters, which I did.

For this course I obtained a laptop, all work, all assignments, all papers were on this laptop. Yep, I know what you are thinking already and at that moment in time, I asked myself that very same question, why did I have all my eggs in that little basket?

Because, despite the history, despite where I worked, I didn't imagine that someone would be that evil, but he was.

That laptop went down the same flight of stairs as my sanctuary, all I can remember saying was 'oh no' repeatedly and crying. But still, I re-did work, I re-got information and I still completed the course.

I no longer have any of the awards physically, they were all destroyed, punched from the frames they were in and ripped to shreds in one of his rages; but that's no surprise to you is it and more fool me for displaying them. Apparently you can obtain them as they are numbered, but what's the point, I've no use for them now, it would be somewhat hypocritical to work in that profession again, besides, I'm too old.

May his decaying heart be tried by the old justice, maybe there's an old judge close by! There most certainly is room for a jury. But that's not really why I did what I did, all the above is really quite trivial, he was far meaner than that.

During the summer months last year I did see Mr Brain tumor from a distance a few times, but avoided and went in another direction; over the winter no one was really about and then we went into another inhibiting lockdown, so I haven't seen him in a long while, maybe he died? Or maybe it's because I've not had a need to go there much lately, I had other places to go.

Did you find lockdown lonely? I have wondered about that. Although I was incredibly busy myself, I was in fact adjusting to literally being on my own. Although it had been my choice, by way of my actions, and I felt like I had taken control for the first time in my life, learning to live without having to obtain permission or having to justify oneself or working around someone else's plans, did initially feel strange. Not hearing someone else's movements, speech, breathing, the stillness; It can have the mind playing tricks. Like I said, I was busy, most of my time was occupied, so I don't know what sort of impact it had on people living alone who had time on their hands.

I did do some project work years ago, in the job; it was to do with people who have to be isolated a lot of the time, not through disease, their unpredictable behaviour and the effects of being placed in the 'locked room', 'seclusion', some of which were padded, some just bare rooms. (the bare were worse as they could still punch and headbutt the walls and cause self injury, the ones with bare floors were idiocy, just saying, but the times I saw people head butt floors would make you sick) Rooms in which one cannot voluntarily leave.

Anyway, loneliness, in case you aren't aware, actually has a place in the brain. An area of the brain that is very active when humans are lonely is the Inferior Temporal Gyrus (ITG) This area is where we process and recall faces. It partakes in processing 'social information'. When we are lonely this area is 'on alert', searching and active, quite spontaneously, trying to find faces to look at!

Another part of the brain, the 'Default Mode Network' (DMN) is a collection of areas that combine when our brain is resting, this is our internal sense of 'me', our identity. All the parts comprising the DMN are in relation to memory and emotion; basically our lives thus far lived, that contributes to our life experiences that have ultimately made us, us, the 'me'.

I wonder if the DMN is responsible for 'mind pops' / 'brain pops' when we find ourselves alone? This may explain why the brain chucks up a random image, a face, a place, a time, a voice and so on. Maybe when the brain is not active enough, it gets lonely? Isolation means your brain is isolated, unless you are constantly feeding it, it's searching and on alert.

When the brain experiences isolation (loneliness) areas activate to seek social encounters, particular neurons called Dorsal Raphe Dopamine Neurons react to loneliness which cause 'seeking' behaviour. In fact, chronic loneliness (over a long period of time) can 're-write' synaptic paths and alter how you view the world, basically it literally can change who you are!

It is thought that the lonely brain is in fact in pain, confused and stressed. So I wonder what impact lockdown had on the lonely and the already lonely; I wonder how many people came out the otherside a different person to that before?

I know I've changed, I see the world completely differently now, but that's not due to loneliness, it's due to the latest of many events in 1 narcissist road.

Who's m-field was the start of all this I cannot tell as I do not know, and the fact that m-fields join and influence another on marriage makes it a ridiculous idea to think one could pinpoint the actual beginning as it would go back hundreds of years, but I do know there was some weird choices of relationships way back, and some terrible acts; did the knowledge of such family secrets influence the minds and behaviours of the subsequent generations? or does it get passed on in the genes?
Do people subconsciously seek out similar minded people?
or is the attachment to do with similar life events?
It is not as straightforward as nature / nurture, as I know I think completely differently to how my siblings did.

My Grandfather, on my dad's side, grew up mostly without the presence of his biological father, who was a bit of a tyrant, he stayed with his mother, who had several male friends after the absence of his father; but at the age of 14 he was sent away to another country to work the land. He was trained here, at a boarding training camp, not far from where I am today, which was run by a religious charity who paid the passage and organised the placements abroad.

I am sure that you are fully aware what happened to these youngsters in the early 1900's sent out as forced labour to countries afar, under the guise of charity. So his story is not great to begin with, then he was sent away to slave labour and abuse and neglect where survival skills were needed beyond what most can imagine as a child. As an adult with his already formed harsh character with a terrible streak of sadistic terror, he became a prisoner of war in WW2, where he apparently came back even worse.

My Grandmother (dad's side) was born into poverty in London, second from youngest, both girls, late arrivals after a bunch of much older boys.

Her mum died, her dad became very ill, her much older brothers (who eventually went away to war) were older enough to fend for themselves.

The girls were taken into care, the youngest stayed in that home much longer but my grandmother at the age of 10 was shipped out to another country to enter domestic labour.

I needn't tell you what she endured as she was passed from placement to placement, pillar to post, all under the famous 'charity' to clear the streets of London of the waifs and strays.

It was a brutal life and many did not survive and many took their own lives. This life did not create a monster in my grandmother, her coping skills were 'acceptance', she accepted that abuse was part of life. She was far too accepting by the time she reached adulthood, but that was not her fault, the only flaw she had was to instill in me that 'these things happen', otherwise to me, she is the bravest person I have ever known or likely to ever know.

These two beings from the same birth country, sent to the same country, by different 'charities' at different times, were both basically sent to be servants, as children.

These two beings met as adults in that country and married; there was 'talk' throughout the years that in her marrying him, it was her way out of service, but I can't vouch for that.

They moved into a log cabin, sounds idyllic doesn't it, but it wasn't, these log cabins were shacks on a lake where poor workers lived, away from the land owners.

I made a telephone call one day, years ago; I wanted to know if the place on my dad's birth certificate was still there. I was given a number to call which turned out to be for the tourist board in that area. I spoke at length to a man who told me about that street and as a tourist attraction, there stands a replica 'log cabin' with the history and what happened in the recession which saw it all decay.
I wanted to know what happened to number '1', I wanted to know if it was still standing, that is why I called.

After my dad died I couldn't find his birth certificate, on talking to the embassy I was given documents to apply to get a copy. It took some weeks and I had to send his death certificate to obtain it, but when it arrived I couldn't believe what I saw. What is it with the number 1?

Anyway, the newlyweds began having babies, many miscarriages and some infant deaths, (some even documented on my dad's birth certificate) my grandmother managed to raise 6, all dead now of course and most before their time.

This is where half the immediate story begins; my grandfather was a cruel and sadistic man, he was brutal. The recession hit that country, my grandmother managed to get work as a cook on a huge farm; she had learnt to cook in her placements and was in fact very good. She obtained work, he did not; it meant he became the minder of the children and babies, and he was mean.
One time he purposely put the baby crib too close to the open fire, the cinders and sparks burnt the baby, the more the baby screamed, the closer to the fire he put the baby, until the oldest child intervened, the second eldest ran to where their mum was working. When she arrived he was in such a rage that he refused to let her in, he threw

stuff out the door at her and there was a major scene, he then left, left her with all the children and he worked his way back to this country on a boat with cattle. Of course this is a very short version of the story of some of my genes.

In those days the form of communication was by letter and that took a long time to get from one country to the next. It transpired that my grandfather went to his sisters once back in this country (the country that he was sent from many years prior as a child) His sister was worried about all the children that he had left behind, who were not citizens of this country by birth.

She wrote to my grandmother and asked her to bring the children, the upshot being that my grandmother, all by herself, came over to this country with all her children, like I said, a brave woman. On arriving with 6 children she then had to make her way down country to her sister-in-laws.

That relationship (my grandparents) picked up where it left off a year earlier; you need to bear in mind that this was after the first world war and just before the second, she had 6 children and no other family and was essentially a foreigner to the country in which she had been born, and of which had betrayed her.

She had nothing and only knew that to survive you need to accept anything and everything.

My father grew up in that environment, harsh to begin with, born abroad into poverty and a brutal father, made brutal from his experiences, made worse by war. Then something even worse happened to my father!

At the age of 13 my father went rabbiting to get food for the table, he set light to the field in an attempt to smoke the rabbits out.

He was caught, he didn't receive a smack upside the head, he was sent to Borstal; to remain there until national service.

Borstal didn't educate boys, they learnt to work and learnt to fight for their lives, many died, many killed themselves.

Do I need to tell you what happened to blonde curly haired boys of 13 that entered borstal?

I don't think so, and if you have no idea what I am referring to, then consider yourself extremely fortunate, ignorance is bliss.

But put it this way, if you woke my father and you were too close, his immediate and involuntary reaction would be to floor you, if he had been drinking, he wouldn't stop until the devil had run. Some things that are so terrible stay with you until you die and maybe, who knows, beyond that even.

My Grandmother on my mother's side had a saying "don't wash your dirty laundry in public" and my other grandmother would say "keep family matters private" but most matters weren't even talked about privately within the family. In fact things would be hushed up pretty quickly, only made reference to on a 'need to know basis', but nothing was really ever dealt with. You heard things, you may have been privy to things but things were left, brushed under the carpet.

One had to learn to live with the effect or the knowledge of a happening that would leave you sick to the stomach; life carried on and you were expected to 'get a backbone', 'don't be spineless', basically get on with it.

This came down the generations and I too passed this on. It wasn't the 'stiff upper lip', it was the ability to dismiss others as long as oneself was ok.

A token gesture of acknowledgment to the event or events, then that's that, done, over, move on.

These coping mechanisms didn't work, it bred selfishness and wiped out the ability to decenter and place yourself in someone else's shoes, it grew a culture of disdain for others and you just simply didn't care. You learnt to not feel deeply for humans with the knowledge that people are fickle and pretty selfish and they will do just about anything in order to survive and are capable of pretty much anything to get what they want.

Can I liken the past and present of these walls to a bunch of heathens? Not quite, but I guess it depends what your understanding of a heathen is.
In the biblical sense, it is someone without religion; my mother's mother believed in Jesus, she wouldn't sew on a sunday as it would prick Jesus's heart, she always wore a cross but her past was immoral.
My grandfather (dad's side) had a lot to do with the salvation army, his brutality and actions toward my grandmother (his wife) at times couldn't be justified by God.
My dad had songs of praise on every sunday, he said it was top of the pops for Jesus; when he was ill he would holler from his room, this was in response to the 'little people' coming out of the cupboard, he asked for a cross. The cross that I gave him from my neck, silver cross and chain, was hung on the wall above his head, it stopped the little people pulling at him.
None of these people lived by the bible but had some affiliation with religion.

Heathen (in slang) is a person who lies, cheats and is immoral in actions; immoral being someone without morals, morals being a lack of standards in behaviour not conforming to right and wrong.

Did we all run around causing mayhem and obtaining police presence? No.

Did we draw attention from the community? No.

In the sense of heathen to the outside world, no, not at all. Clean, tidy, polite people.

What went on behind closed doors was a different matter; a family matter.

Not all of us share the same traits, not everyone was a liar, the lying, cheating trait was mainly bought into the family, not our genetics; I could not call my dad a liar or a cheat, nor his parents, nor his siblings, they were so adamant that they were right all the time that they had no need to tell a lie; their belief in their own belief didn't give rise to the need to lie.

They always had their reasons for their actions, only my grandmother understood all of them.

From boys to men they were polite, yes mam, no sir, but all ruled their roosts with brutality. Discipline and control, I guess the walls saw dysfunctional moral standards, personal perceptions of right and wrong, not acceptable to this day and age; as I said earlier, years ago my actions may have just been accepted as justified.

Years ago domestic violence wasn't a crime, beating your kids until they were black and blue wasn't a crime. An Englishman's home was his castle, the police would leave the property if ordered off. Morals only really came about due to religion; so what I'm saying is, It's complicated.

But at the end of the day the only way to look at it is, if your actions have wilfully inflicted pain on another, without justification, then it is wrong; it is cruel and selfish to harm another for no good reason or to satisfy your own needs.

1 Narcissist Road only saw a few actual heathens.

In case you are envisaging (have a mental picture of) 1 narcissist road as some run down, poverty stricken, drugs and drink dwelling with filthy uneducated slobs, this is not the case. Everyone worked, clothed, fed, clean, tidy, cars, pets, holidays and just so you know, times of celebration and laughter; fix your image to something more akin to a normal family in your street. Now stop and think, how well do you know that family?

When the door is shut do you know for a fact what goes on in that house?
Of course you don't, you see what people allow and want you to see, it's as simple as that.
But having said that, times have changed as have policy and law, so maybe in this day and age some happengings are detectable; there are places of refuge for those brave enough to break free, however, there is still room for improvement. As we are aware, victims aren't always believed; we are still old fashioned in that we still have ruling royalty, a society aimed at the rich benefiting above the worker bees; a country taking draconian steps backwards in time, but that's another story.

I'm saying that what is not considered acceptable now, some of it was when i was growing up, and back then it would have caused shame to admit to an outsider what had happened for some years, it was bad enough telling my mother; the silence was only broken on this 'need to know basis' secret due to biology and I had reached an age of awareness.

But on thinking about it right now, have things changed?
If it was the current time, would I tell today?

At the risk of not being believed, tearing families apart, courts, being looked at differently, being treated differently, it being common knowledge?

I'm not sure I am brave enough to place that happening out of context into this current time and I have trouble with reliving some deep traumas, it wasn't dealt with appropriately by anywhere near nowadays standards; it could be easier to seek help today, but I cannot put myself into those shoes again, I offer no advice.

But I will tell you that it contributed to how I ended up in this situation today, and you don't want that do you. At the end of the day, you have an option, I hope.

But anyway, I believe that to take someone's life, you don't have to physically kill them; however, I did find it was easier and far less time consuming with relatively little effort.

I don't know if you are aware of how different your life will be in a few years time?

Do you know that committing a crime in the near future will be easily detectable?

Which is why I'm glad that I did what I did, when I did. Had it of been now with no lockdown and better knowledge of the 'virus', disposals would have been very tricky; but in the future it would have been impossible.

We think that being watched means CCTV or location on our phones; we do cash exchanges, cash in hand, the dark web, speak in person, make deals in pubs; on the whole we aren't literally being watched. But things have begun to exist and spy on our lives, but it is to become far more than that.

I didn't know until recently that the cameras on the self scan was clocking my face and that even though I was wearing a mask, it knows exactly who I am, neither was I aware that the itemised till receipts are kept and the bank card used could be pulled up to see exactly what I buy and when; this knowledge has led me to use cash only in such places, but of course cash is being phased out so there's no way out of it in the long run. Who would have thought that your spending habits would be used in the not so distant future to aid you in making healthy choices and influence your access to health facilities.

DIGITAL ID: CONTROL: PANOPTICON:

On investing this invasion of privacy, I was shocked to discover the proposed plans for our future; the integrated digital portfolio that will integrate our finances, banking, what we owe and to whom, our income, credit score, what we spend on and where, our healthy choices or not, our health status, our immunisations, our past, present and our predicted future.

Every person born will have a global ID which will permit our movements or not, we will be dictated to and denied, earning permission.

I also discovered the internet panopticon and how we will be continuously watched and monitored; we can be viewed on our cameras on our devices, listened to via our microphones. We already knew that voice command devices are listening in, that is common knowledge.

Drones will watch us from the sky whilst platforms with QR codes will see us from shop windows, public transport, public buildings. We will ping off everywhere we go, it is being implemented as I write, so I suggest you start to tie up those loose ends pretty soon.

I've read articles about people going off grid and how to do it, it is appealing and as they say, 'the less you have, the less complicated your life becomes'; however, I cannot see that it would be very easy, how would one survive? Being self-sufficient would require land ownership and one would need access to healthcare at some point and it is unlikely that this will be permitted; the impossibilities of escaping!

One has to be careful with the internet, but I'm sure you are aware already; if you type something in the search bar, before you know it you get an advert. But what's coming is deeper than this.
Like i said, I have to go soon, before I'm part of the track and trace, before the vaccinations become mandatory, before they can look at who I am and who I'm with and before they restrict movements out of the country again, as they will and you can be sure it will not be to do with a virus.
Their intention is to halt us, pause us, digitise us, document and cloud us, before we have the 'perception' of freedom again. I say perception as in reality, we will never be actually free again. It's over, the old way of life, it's gone, it's not coming back, there will be a new living reality, one that's watched and dictated. The New World.
I'm lucky, I realise that already, and not only have I ended generational trauma, but I had the opportunity to succeed in keeping this private; and I had the opportunity to discover what is coming, therefore the opportunity to get out now and start a new life, not completely off grid, but I will be away from here nonetheless.
Most people spend their lives with heads down, unaware of the road ahead; my head was down the whole of my life, a spontaneous act led me to look straight ahead; the subsequent knowledge gained has me looking miles ahead now, and far more knowledgeable than I had ever considered possible.

Initially I was concerned about my medical records being some sort of a connection but after changing my GP surgery twice, I realised that no one had the time or need to even question why and in the last move they haven't even got the information on my childhood vaccinations or had knowledge of a particular health happening some years back; it appears that things are currently a mess and institutions don't communicate, so there is no need for concern there.

Once the digital ID is in place, everything about you will be on it, medical records will be easy to access, maybe the current chaos is to do with that.

However, once I've actually left the country it won't actually matter anyway; and yes, I am lucky that my dad was born abroad, it gave me citizenship to two countries, but I cannot go there directly from here; I'm going elsewhere first.

Was this knowledge in the subconscious, being that it is more intelligent than we are aware of, did it know that I had an escape route I wonder.

Likewise, I considered my credit file, presently it is irrelevant unless one wanted credit; electoral roll is only required if one wishes to vote; did I lie on the census?

No I did not, I simply put that it was just me living here on that particular day in time, and it was true as all body parts were gone, they didn't live here anymore; the census is silly anyway, a ten year snapshot, it doesn't mean one was here before nor after, an irrelevant nonsensical waste of time funds.

I had already dealt with dissociation many months prior; I had access to and knowledge of all passwords for important things. When couples part, as long as everything is tidy, clean, cut and dried, closed, then that's the end of that.

Things can be done online, cleared up, shut down; being in lockdown and restrictions, some facilities were only available online as in person wasn't possible.

I am thankful they sent me lockdown.

Being 'separated' sets you free, if you have no joint accounts, you have no association, that party becomes irrelevant to anything you do subsequently; car insurance, bank account, and the house was never his anyway.

My passports are my own. The past doesn't need to affect your present and future document wise. All I will need to do is pay all bills, close all accounts, close the door, drive away.

Let me just say here, I'm not having the vaccine here, I can still move about with a negative result. This won't be the case eventually, vaccines will become mandatory, they will incorporate it into the new global ID passport, which will begin as a healthpassport in every country. It will show your medical details and it will aid in predicting your health future. So I need to be elsewhere in order to be vaccinated (but only if it becomes mandatory); there's still plenty of time as every pharmaceutical company is in a profit race to bring in all things 'virus' related and vaccination campaigns are going to run for a couple of more years; **my window of opportunity will close by autumn here**, so as I've said, to synchronise this confession with departure does have a time frame.

By the time I'm chipped and tracked I will be in a new life and not looking over my shoulder again; what will that feel like I wonder, it must be great to be 'normal', well as normal as one can be from here on in.

To be honest, there's no such thing as normal, people are all individuals; the normal comes from the norm of a given society, the behaviour of living that is expected and accepted in that given society / culture. Look at the slight difference between the USA and the UK, similar expectations but it is normal behaviour to wave a gun around in the states, not in the UK. That is just one small example obviously, that's not the point, when I say I wish to know what it feels like to feel normal, I probably mean that I wish I had been born to a happy family surrounded by love and protection and nurtured into adulthood with opportunities and support and be part of the brady bunch. Not trauma, abuse, sadness, anxiety, brutality that only ends in detachment, mistrust, deception, disengagement where the restrictions of a 'pandemic' have no negative effects on your life as that type of living was already in practice. (isolation)

There were no family or friends to be parted from, just the one captor as it's offspring was rarely on the scene. So the only effect that lockdown had was, it was the one stone that killed two birds, otherwise there was no one else to miss; hugging your relatives meant nothing to me.

The normal I would like to experience is to go to sleep peacefully with nothing on my mind, nothing to be waiting to happen or expect to happen, not to be filled with dread where you know something will occur but you're not quite sure when; without the expectation of something bad, without fear, with nothing to hide, a normal where one doesn't bear the weight of secrets, knowledge of bad happenings, nightmares and mind pops.

Will I ever lead a life so far removed from this that I will strike up a conversation, invite people home to tea, have friends and partake in activities?

Will it be possible to say I am me, I have no family, I never married or gave birth?

I've not thought that far ahead, all I know is that unless I leave and make a go of it, I will never know.

What happened, happened for a reason, as under normal circumstances I would not be a free woman right now; I've been given an opportunity, therefore, I have to take it. So if I use the word 'normal' in that context again, you will know my meaning.

As human beings, no one from 1 narcissist road could be termed normal; dysfunctional, deranged, insane, warped, was expected to be accepted. At a young age I was privy to the knowledge that my grandfather had done something so horrific to my grandmother that I do believe it messed my mind up enough to of warranted counselling without anything that went on to happen to me after.

As it was a 'family matter' no outsiders were involved, therefore being female, I was part of the care. He had inflicted upon her a sadistic brutal act of inserting a large object into her repeatedly in a violent manner; she was badly hurt and I had never seen so much blood. I was a child, she was a person that I loved. It took me years to understand why she had spent her whole life accepting and excusing people, I don't think she nor my mother realised the life long effect that knowledge had on me and I don't fully understand why, later on, they acted the same way when I had to tell.

Was it because they had experience and their coping was acceptance?

With my grandmother, probably yes, I think so, but not my mother. Anyway, there we are, a brief insight into some sick and twisted.

One of my father's brother's chucked himself in front of a lorry, he was mentally unstable to begin with, far worse after with the brain damage. He attacked his own daughters who were then sent to live at our house; during their long stay, the eldest was preyed upon by another unmarried brother (her own uncle), who had an interest in her so bad that it drove him round the twist and was banned from the house. He ended up crippled after chucking himself on some live electrics that he was meant to be working on.

Another brother, well, where do I begin? He married a lovely lady, she was really kind, I walk past her grave frequently. She became pregnant, he was mean to her, told her to get on with it, made her go to work and see to his needs; she died, it was a bad pregnancy, he didn't believe her when she said she was unwell, she and the baby died.

That was a horrible time, I also remember all the arguments and accusations, which were true; he went off and hung himself from a tree but was found by a passerby before death, despite it being quite out of the way. He was put into a mental ward for a while but later on met and married another lady.

She was divorced and had a child. In our teens, me and my younger brother went with our mother to babysit the child and the new baby; the mother was at work, he was due to go. The child wasn't acting as he should (according to my uncle) he tied the child to a chair and put a wooden block in his mouth; the baby, his baby, was the only being that counted in his life. Another time we turned up early and we heard the thrashing that that child received, this was a long angry viscous thrashing of a child of 4. The story short, the mum left with her child but was denied the baby, he threatened to kill her and given all history, she left without her baby in order to save her child.

That baby grew up thinking she had been abandoned by a bad mother that didn't care about her, far from the truth. But it was all kept in the family.

That baby grew up and married a much older friend of the father's, such things only fitting to this family.

The oldest girl that came to stay at ours, belonging to the other uncle, who was the object of another uncle's affection, relocated to another country, she too used that route of citizenship elsewhere to escape.

Despite the era of non existent domestic abuse and child abuse, these happenings were still very much out of place wouldn't you say. To know all these things were wrong, even though you were growing up in an environment unlike your mates from school. Then they were very abnormal. Had we presented at school as unkempt from non working households, would we have been investigated? Probably not even back then. Many years later, mine weren't investigated either, presenting well and articulate.

The only investigation at school was for the teacher that smacked the spawn of satan, of whom I refused to take it any further as that older, experienced teacher had been driven to distraction and I knew exactly what pushed her to be unprofessional.

If I knew it was possible, I would say that she was lying before she could talk. She came out screaming and never shut up thereafter, she played people like fiddles and ruled the air in any room she frequented.

The entire school age span of years was a constant round of being called and called in, never for violence, not enough to be excluded, just constant goading and disruption, gathering followers along the way.

Manipulation skills of an assassin, she loved nothing more than taking down a victim of her choosing or those that crossed her; it was a challenge of which she would win every single time, setting out to destroy, she would sit back and revel in the downfall, there's a word for that; Schadenfreude (pronounced shaa duhn fray duh)

It was termed to describe someone who enjoys seeing others suffer, they rejoice in others misfortune or achieved by being the target; they revel in witnessing the fall, they gloat over the enemies decline from popularity and in tearing them apart, they feel satisfaction maliciously; a similar term being Epicaricacy.
This is a fitting description of the spawn of satan, she was born from evil genes, made worse by her environment. Her combination of genes and her m-fields were the perfect conditions to grow an expert in character assassination. She had outstanding skills in manipulation and would focus her efforts on deliberate sustained attacks.

I realised this from her first target, her older brother, she did everything and anything to get him into trouble, not like normal sibling rivalry, she continued this at school and would have her followers goad him until he reacted; she would laugh at his punishment received as a consequence of his actions, at school and at home (but not from me).
She played adults one off against the other, teacher against teacher. It could be said that I was a little afraid of what she may come out with next and what would happen if that target ever became me.
It was easier and more comfortable to give in to her than confrontation, looking back I guess that what I was doing was keeping her quiet; she pretty much blackmailed the family members. Without anyone ever having a conversation about it or her, we all

must have known that she was more than capable of blowing the lid off the family secrets, she was never really one of us; she had come into the family and predominantly carried genes from his side, she was the 'cuckoo in the nest'.

I put her heart somewhere that would contain that malicious soul of hers and maybe teach her a few lessons in what evil is like on the receiving end. Nothing in this town has much meaning connected to her, at 18 she up and left, went overseas where she stayed for 15 years. It was only due to her actions in that country that had her run from there; obviously her skills declined with age and she went a step too far.
Her behaviours turned violent and she was incarcerated, when out on probation she fled the country. She had had the intelligence to maintain her passport and returned via the name she went out on; the fact that it had changed due to marriage didn't matter, she never took citizenship, she kept her passport updated from the country she came. It seems to me that she always had an escape plan. Why would you do that if you had married and for all tense and purposes, be settled. What a strange thing to do, clever nonetheless.

The first time it returned here after 15 years, I got the shock of my life. It was a beast, not the skinny 18 year old that had left pretty much as a child; however, even that initial disappearing act must have taken some planning. No one was any the wiser of that until that day the note was left on her bed. "Dear mum, I've left, don't worry about me, I'm safe". That was it.

She had taken very little with her and the room sat in situ for some time. She had even removed the harddrive from the computer in her room. Skills learnt from her father and brother (like I said, all educated here, this was years ago) She was classed as an adult at 18, she had waited 2 weeks after her 18th birthday; aided by mobile phones and internet, it was relatively easy. A few weeks later I received a phone call from a male with an accent. 17 years older than her, in a good job, they had gotten married.

All the programs she watched on satellite tv growing up, even before the dishes that went on the wall, these houses had huge dishes in the garden to which you had to reposition the LNB and dish to get a different channel; then the motorised dishes appeared and the gardens would like like a station trying to pick up activity from extraterrestrials. The kids watched programmes from abroad way before most of their peers; she wanted that life, blue skies, sandy beaches, fast cars, bigger, better, modern; she wanted it, she found a way to get it and went. Things weren't even as technically clever as they are today, this was pre-facebook, pre-twitter, but there were chat boards and forums and no internet panopticon.
Her actions required intelligence, focus and will; unlike me, she didn't have Stockholm syndrome!
Of course initially I did have thoughts of concern, but time passes and one adapts to living in the absence of others and it became somewhat of a relief to be honest. Life without the wake of her scheming and wants became a bit easier, one less duty to occupy my time, life went on, things happened, time ticked by.
Then one day, there she was, like a whirlwind of destruction, I can't even say a re-surfacing as this 'being' returned far worse than the one that left, twice the size, far taller than me, and violent.

She didn't hang around too long, most of us had died or relocated in her long absence, basically all she wanted was money, somewhere to stay whilst she plotted her next move. She went and changed her name again would you believe; she changed her birth name completely, had me get it verified by a publican, take her to the passport office on a one day turnaround facility and of course had me pay. Armed with this new passport and money and change of haircut and clothes; she was gone again, this time mainland europe. This time was a sigh of relief and I hoped it would be another 15 years before she darkened the doorstep again.

I hope that you realise that I'm just filling you in on the very short versions, I don't wish to drag it all out, too long and laborious. Anyway, she went, however, she returned unexpectedly, less than a year later, a few months into lockdown. Now tell me, how did she manage to do that? She said it was easy, came in by ferry and no one checked as she was returning home; this was before any of the so-called testing was being carried out. She then came here via train, well shocked is an understatement, I was actually thrown. Her observations that her dad and one dog were missing didn't take but 15 minutes, but I remember it feeling like the longest pause in history and having massive heart palpitations.
I think that is the only time in my life that I really knew what fear felt like, the fight or flight was massive in response. I had been through some things in my life that had scared me, but this was 100% fear, fear of being found out, caught.
In a split second I involuntarily acted on the 'next time do it better'. I'm not sure if it was due to it being my offspring, but unlike before, I went from behind, she didn't see it coming, her last sight was not me, unlike his; I wonder if that was some unconscious compassion, maybe I didn't really want to do it, who knows?

But she left me no choice, like i said, us humans will do anything to survive. It was me or her, I chose me. I'm guessing you are shocked, but maybe not; the offspring was evil and had left at 18, I've no idea who this being was that had turned up after all those years, I didn't like that person, but I wouldn't have gone out my way to take it out; it came back here uninvited, sticking it's nose in and would have chucked me under the bus in a blink of an eye. It wasn't my fault.

But this time, unlike the previous time, I had no idea where she had been or who with or if she had told anyone where she was going. I had no knowledge of banks, passwords, emails or indeed social media. I assumed considering she had left that first country whilst awaiting sentencing that she didn't have a social media account and that she didn't have long standing contacts; my assumption was and is, being someone on the run, one doesnt plant their face all over the internet. Having said that, I've no idea who she knows or who she talks to; maybe no one of any importance, no one close, as if there had of been, she wouldn't have come back here.

At least with him I pretty much had all knowledge and knew everything that there was to know of importance. I was fully aware that he didn't have any close friends, he had pissed them all off over the years, any new acquaintances didn't matter.

Everyone around here was already aware that it wasn't uncommon for him to leave for periods of time. He had done this from day one, he would leave and return. He would have what I termed his 'fashions of the moment', he would attach himself to a pub or club, get involved then after a while he would turn the 'act' off, fall out with people and never go back there again; so I was certain that no one would miss him and if asked, all I had to say was that he had left again, but given that it was a common occurrence, no one asked then and still haven't.

He wasn't working, he did that a lot, he had walked out of his last job, just like all the rest, had an argument, got into a rage and walked. He had pretty much run out of options here anyway.

With her, unlike him, I had no idea if she had a phone simm, was on a contract, pay as you go or just using wifi; I didn't know if it was a simm for here or from where she had been; or if in fact she had even been out of the country at all.

She may have been here all along, with her one never knew truth from lie. So I turned that phone off. Three days later I drove out of town via the country roads; I went quite a long way without being pulled over, waved down or anything. I took the dog and if I had of been stopped I would have not argued, I would have accepted the fine for leaving town in lockdown, it was a risk worth taking. All they would have found was an older woman and a dog gone a bit stir crazy in lockdown as she lives alone, and I would have been very sorry.

I turned the phone on when I got near the airport; I had actually taken that route before when the motorway had been closed due to an accident, the older sibling was a taxi driver before he died; this route was common knowledge to those in the trade. Anyway, not far from there I turned the phone back on, sat in the layby a while, then smashed it to smithereens in a bag with my hammer that I had stuffed up inside the passenger seat where the dog sat.

Call this paranoid if you like, but I did consider that if someone somewhere reported her missing and one could actually be traced via one's phone, then the last location of the signal would show near the airport. Given her history, no one would be surprised. Then bit by bit, tiny pieces were disposed of in the garbage ridden hedgerows whilst walking my dog for his needs and stretching his little legs.

The rest went into the dog poop bag, I drove into the village, found a dog poop bin and disposed of all traces to go off to the incinerator. I drove home, satisfied I had done the best thing, I then had to complete what I had started.

I only ever drove out of town one more time during a lockdown, but nowhere near as far away; but I had to, our level of restrictions were not like before, it meant that many more people were out and about. I had to get a chest freezer and keep it in my room 'for dog meat' for a while; it was too busy and what had happened with that first lodger wasn't meant to happen. I am pretty sure that there were 5 times as many dog walkers than before even the first lockdown, there seemed to be a million new puppies being paraded about like some sort of lockdown trophy. Far too many people milling around the old haunts; I told you this lodger was trouble, even so after death.
In and around town wasn't safe this time round, I had to go out of town. Thankfully I had had dogs for years and knew where to go, it was the when which was tricky. My 3rd and hopefully my last need for disposal had been prepared with expertise, I had perfected everything so that the subsequent lodgers had no idea what had gone on before their arrival nor what was in my freezer in my room; but considering I had a fridge in there and a kettle, it didn't appear out of place. Due to the virus, all responsible precautions were taken. No items of cutlery or crockery were shared, separate fridge and freezers; separate toilets even; the use of communal cooking was rare, we had separate microwaves, so no, it wasn't a strange happening to separate things, it was responsible behaviour.

Did it bother me that at night I knew what was in the freezer under those loaves of bread that I would never eat?
A bit yes, for the simple reason it was unfinished business.

Why did I re-let the rooms with the evidence in the house still? Because to me it showed that there was nothing to hide and if anyone came investigating, the rooms were occupied, yeah he was here for about a week but then up and left without notice; but as suspected, on one has come by.

I don't even know where he came from or if the name he gave was his real name, I doubt it. All I'm going to say about him or that is, the trees are many, the area vast and is of royal connection. One can spend a day there and still manage to get lost. On two returns to my car I was a few miles off, one of which I had to walk the road to get back to the car; on one time of trying to return to the car to fill the backpack I got disorientated and I saw the same tree marked 111 four times; very tricky and clearly a negative sense of direction.

I guess at this point you are wondering how I physically disposed of them. I don't wish to be graphic nor give any sick and twisted individual any ideas. Neither do I wish to write a step by step guide in body dismemberment or dismemberment for dummies; I'm pretty sure that cannot be legal. However, having said that, textbooks for becoming an anatomical pathologist aren't illegal, it is relatively easy to obtain the information on how to dissect / dimember; but only someone lacking intelligence would type that into a search engine. As mentioned previously, where I said it takes one to recognise one; the career I studied for and worked in for several years has a shelf life, picking up some of those traits blended well with those obtained from the family environment, but it was in fact fuel to the fire.

Forensic mental health, secure hospitals for those whose criminal offence saw them incarcerated in special secure psychiatric 'hospitals' instead of prison. Quite why they term them hospitals I don't know, as the vast majority are untreatable and it is simply a matter of containment. Working with such individuals and reading their files can damage the mind of any person; it can also feed the mind of warped persons and I worked with several of those in that professional capacity. This field of mental health is a whole different ball game, the people that wind up working this sector will either go mad and become deranged or swing completely the other way and become detached; but this detachment isn't just in the working environment, you have to have an element of detachment from all people. Once you learn in depth the capabilities of humans, you realise that any individual can turn on a sixpence and act upon another in ways not thought possible of that person before. (I did) You also come to realise that we are all not so different and I have already proved that it isn't always possible to keep control and display restraint, we are all capable of 'snapping', maybe detaching keeps that at bay.

Having said that, as of course you are aware, it isn't just about 'snapping' on a one off occasion; there are those whose behaviours are ongoing, long term, untreatable, dangerous. Being involved with these cases meant that you were privy to some god awful information. However, there are enough books out there to feed the curious mind, I was reading them before I even commenced studies. Many people read these books as a form of entertainment, likewise there are movies.

What makes us read these books and watch these movies?

Why do we want to know what they did, how they did it and to whom?

Is it due to curiosity or some need for psychological excitation, do we take pleasure in learning the nasty specifics?

the shock facto? or is it to gain some understanding as to why?

Why did I have an interest in such behaviours when I was already aware of sick behaviour, I should have been repulsed; so I guess I was seeking the why.

Having read most books on the market and those required for study, I was already aware of failings in attempting to cover up crimes; I did bear this in mind and of course I already had some inside, albeit second hand knowledge of how people get caught.

Some people have done the stupidest of things; there was a chap that bludgeoned his mother to death with a heavy ashtray but then carried on using it after cleaning it, he said he kept it as he needed it. Whilst working in this sector I did gain an understanding that not all of these people are bad, but their behaviour had been.

'He' used to say, how can you work with those specimens, why can't you get an ordinary job, yours is embarrassing.

I could tell him now that they taught me well, but I doubt he'd hear me, too busy being force fed contaminated beer; I wonder if it ever crossed his mind that it would contribute to his end and eternal purgatory. Maybe he burnt those books for a reason!

Speaking of bad behaviour, I've seen some really bad behaviour from staff that I worked with. I myself was never unprofessional but some were; I'm not talking about those that reacted wrongly, say in an act of self defence; it's easy to think that all the training you have to pass prepares you for events, but it doesn't. You do what you have to do to get out of a predicament. If you are being attacked and your radio / alarm has gone out of reach, are you expected to just take a sustained attack and hope you survive?

That goes against the human instinct to survive does it not; you involuntarily do what you have to do and sometimes this may involve protecting yourself or even running if you could to get away!

It's a tricky situation and sometimes the unpredictable happens, the most experienced staff still get taken by surprise.

Staff shortages contributed to unsafe environments, unsafe for both staff and residents; I've seen residents attack residents, the intervention takes more than one staff member. I've seen all hell break loose and seen many people get hurt; there's no easy simple answer when all control has been lost. The strength of some is impossible to deal with and the environments aren't always appropriate.

There's a fine line between treating people like humans whereby their surroundings require access to 'normal' items, than to those items being used inappropriately and becoming weapons, a danger to others or self.

It's ok for an establishment to permit something, as the decision makers make the decisions from their offices, in order to keep in line with standards and policy; and until something occurs that shows that that person is likely to use it inappropriately, then these situations continue to happen.

It doesn't affect the office dwellers, they don't really know the people either, snapshot reports, brief history, piss poor risk assessments, they never get harmed or put into or deal with situations. They don't care, they are simply complying with policies.

Pool cues, pool / snooker balls (these hurt a lot) tv's, tv aerials, bats (but it's ok as it's a soft ball), dvd's, cd's, pens, pencils, paper with staples, rulers, chairs & tables not fixed to the floor, board games with counters & figures, electronic items, dart boards with velcro darts, crockery, cutlery and personal hygiene items, clothes hangers ect.

One can spend much time clearing out a room after an incident whilst another risk assessment takes place as to the risk of the room's content, only to put it all back again.

It depends on the type of establishment you are working for; the worst being where individuals don't have contact with others, just staff, there are also differing levels in the 'secure', I am sure you are all aware of the three high-security psychiatric hospitals.
These are a different entity, a bit like Biosecurity level 4 one could say. But I have no knowledge of these.

My first experience of a secure psychiatric setting was at the age of 15, it was the summer I went elsewhere before the courts brought me back.
The hospital grounds were secured by a high fence, but there were parts of it that could be viewed by walking through some woods; I was shown it for fun. This is where the kids would spit into the grounds and make fun of those walking around, some staff weren't much better, they would laugh at the kids. The mother of the family I was staying with worked there, she would tell how so & so had to be tied to the pillar for whatever reason that day. The pillar being the marble type pillars in the large rooms of the victorian type building; who got the cold bath, cold shower, who didn't get any food and so on. I didn't like any of this talk and didn't find any of it funny. I didn't dislike them because of it. I considered that they thought differently, they weren't bad people, it was their 'normal', they didn't think of those people as being people, they were nutters who were locked up.
But that was a long time ago now, perceptions have moved on a bit since, but my recollection of those people that I saw through the fence is that they were of low functioning, not thinking calculating persons, being of where I ended up making a career in.
In this environment you still get some staff that gain amusement and some that take out their frustrations, crossing that professional boundary.

I've seen some goad and torment, be overzealous on intervention and some be downright cruel. It is understandable that the occasional staff breakdown, where their emotions are expressed verbally and the periodic, at wit's end shout of 'oh just f off', followed by a nervous laugh and an apology with the excuse of having a bad day. In this day and age, even those falldown moments would be classed as abuse. How the hell most of those botched control and restraints were ever gotten away with I don't know, the average joe with no training could have drawn conclusion from merely observing that it was just wrong and abusive.

I hope you've never witnessed someone face down with arms and legs crossed over their back with people holding tight to all limbs and head. The more the person struggled and moved (due to all air being restricted) the longer they were held. Maybe you have knowledge of these holds going terribly wrong, it is atrocious; these were approved holds for restraining people, designed i am sure by some sick individuals, lunatics in the wrong job.
The attitude back then was to control the situation with the least amount of staff being hurt; situations arose where nervous staff would jump too quick and the resident would be on the floor before you could blink and the resident hadn't even done anything; they may have frowned or moved too quick and that nervous staff member stopped something from happening that may never have even happened.

If someone jumped you, what would your reaction be? Exactly, you would respond with self defence right? When this happened, for nothing, the resident would end up being restrained by a team of staff for reacting to the nervous staff's actions of knocking them to the floor.

An avoidable situation yet unavoidable when staff became 'jumpy'. Tricky environment like I've said, one needed nerves of steel, fortunately for me I did. Obtained by frequent beatings growing up and on marriage. To me, getting smacked about was relatively normal, I was desensitised, it didn't bother me, but having said that, I was rarely attacked at work.

It wasn't because I sat in an office out of the way, I was on the floor, maybe I was invisible back then too. I did get injured a couple of times, but I wasn't the target, it was on intervention; many things happen in chaotic moments before control is achieved.

Radios bounce away, panic buttons get smashed, keys for the locked doors get ripped from around the staff necks (yes people really were that stupid) punches get thrown in the wrong direction, people get bitten, kicked, heads smack into floors and walls, residents get agitated and join in on occasions and before you know it, it's a free for all; blood, mucus everywhere, much heavy breathing, clothes ripped, footwear lost, hair pulls everywhere, rolling around on the floor, you needed to be fit and have stamina to survive; like I said, the job has a shelf life.

Sometimes on the odd occasion, a resident would take revenge on a staff that had wronged them. The event may have taken place weeks before, but then suddenly an opportunity arises. I heard of some, I witnessed a couple; one time sticks in my head probably as I thought it was genius. The resident asked for the paper that they had been given (with some info on it) to be laminated, but before it was laminated he wanted particular words underlined.

This all happened so quickly; he didn't ask me, he bypassed me to that male staff.

He was quite clever as he did it all so fast; when that staff member went into the office to get a pen the resident said, give me the pen I'll do it myself, the expected answer being, no, you know you can't, just show me. So he pointed out the first word, it was underlined, the second, it was underlined, on the third word that pen was whipped up out of the staff's hand and plunged down, straight through the hand holding the paper flat. Right through his hand it went, there he was, Mr macho, jumping up and down screaming with a pen sticking out his hand.

The resident stood and waited for the intervention, he didn't resist and lay face down grinning. I guess he thought the revenge was worth the coming punishment. No pens out the office meant no pens out the office, but complacency sets in, people get caught, the rules are adhered to for a while after.

I've seen staff coated in hot meals, hot coffee, bowls of soup. I've seen staff coated in feces and spit and urine. One should take care in their approach to residents, they are usually in there for a reason. Obviously they have capabilities or they wouldn't be in there would they, so why aggravate, goad, smirk at, delay permission to the bathroom, ignore or be cruel intentionally?

The objective was to control the environment, not to control the individual all of the time; stick a tiger in a cage but expect to be bitten on entering no?

What is considered justifiable and proportionate revenge anyway? Isn't it a bit like asking how much something is worth when the item is of sentimental value; justifiable and proportionate is surely in the eye of the beholder, subjective. When you hear people talk of 'over reaction', does it not make you question from where the 'rules' of reaction come from?

There aren't any are there, as it's all down to subjective perception; I don't think I overreacted in doing what I did. They were actions from within reacting to situations, the alternative of doing nothing and sitting idly by, would have had negative consequences.

We react how we react at that moment in time via instructions from within, the subconscious, being smarter than we realise; so next time someone tells you you've overreacted, ask them says who?

But I guess it depends on the outcome of that 'overreaction'; a reaction would usually be thought of as in that moment of a happening that one immediately responds to, spontaneous; if one reacts much later on, that then becomes revenge.

However, reacting to an immediate situation in which there is history between the parties, can influence that reaction, as it did with me.

It was one time too many, I took that spontaneous opportunity to end it, get revenge and I aimed all those wasted years and his cruelty to the kids, right at the front of his head, then again, right in the face. He saw it coming but wasn't expecting it, he didn't have time to react.

The first blow was enough to knock him off his feet, the second kept him down, the third was just one for luck; in which I held both handles as I couldn't get a one handed swing to easily aim at the top of his head as he was on the floor, I had to straddle him to do that.

The Doufeu is a heavy beast, large oval cast iron; the handle on each side only allows for 3 fingers, swinging it required a hook action which actually strained my wrist and it hurt a lot after; when I used it on her from behind I used both hands and came down hard at the base of her head which was painful on the fingers and I did drop it, the impact jerked back my arms, it wasn't with ease.

I knew that a hard blow to the region of the occipital meeting the atlas vertebra would highly likely cause rapid death. Destroying relay signals from the brain to the body to breath and the heart to pump, cutting off the arteries supplying oxygenated blood to the brain; an internal decapitation.

Swift and I'm assuming, painless, the action was successful. There wasn't really a thought of 'cop that you evil being', just relief with the added bonus of the knowledge that she would never destroy another nor would I be in fear of her trying to hunt her parents down on return in the future only to find neither.

Did I ever consider that I was capable of ending the life of another? I hadn't really given it in depth thought; small acts of revenge at home was the norm, I had thought many times "I'll effing kill you one day" in respect to several family members, but I'd never dwelled on it nor sat and planned it.

I'd worked with so-called killers, read much stuff, studied some, but it wasn't planned in advance until the third time.

It is generally thought that to terminate another in such a way and to dismember and dispose of, that one would need to dehumanise the individual. But in my humble (no one important) opinion, especially in respect to the first, dehumanisation would be pointless if one's aim is to gain some satisfaction from the knowledge that they are aware of your actions.

The fact that they know what you are about to do, is half the point in doing it.

Likewise, she didn't dehumanise did she, the whole point of her actions was that they knew what she was doing; so there we are, motivation and a deadly agenda to which she gained much pleasure, now at an end.

All those years I wasted makes me angry now, I wasn't before, just frustrated. Now that I'm out of it all, not held by anyone's m-field, as they're all dead, I look back and question my 'self sabotage'. If your life bears the slightest resemblance to my past, then maybe you should think about it, what is it you are waiting for?
No one is coming to save you, save yourself; cut the ties that bind. Just saying.
Easy for me to say now, but look what had to occur before I bust through that invisible forcefield. Tainted from the past of which I admit I was a conscious co-creator; why I waited so long I don't know in all honesty.
I'm now so desensitised that cutting up three bodies didn't affect me that much, physically the smell was sickening and vile, mentally nothing, not even now, nothing.
Just as well isn't it or else my new life would be ruined.

As I've said, I don't think it appropriate to give a step by step guide. The hardest part was getting two dead weights up the stairs, the third was already up there.
I eventually learnt with the first that they needed to be wrapped in water proof to begin with or else you get a trail of unpleasantries; then a king size duvet to put them in and I used loft boards for the stairs, the car's tow rope around the top of the bannister made the task far easier. Don't get me wrong, it wasn't easy, it was hard work but from the top of the stairs the bathroom is the first door on the landing.
Burning clothes and burnable possessions took a while (the rest went into boxes in the loft with the other stuff initially) It isn't uncommon around this semi-rural area to have fires, almost a daily occurrence. But my fire pit was pretty much destroyed in the end, the heat off some things was phenomenal.

Dried garden foliage and quick light logs aided by liquid nicotine used for vaping! One pound for a small bottle gives the fire umph. I didn't use petrol as that is dangerous and it smells, I did use some items from the internet that I obtained from some pagan websites, herbs, barks, resins, blends, oils (none of these purchases draw attention) not only did they burn extremely well, which is their intended purpose, but the pleasant fragrances helped to overpower any unwanted odors. I used them indoors and out, they worked really well; but I will say that these places don't always have warnings against these products.

One time I do believe I got as high as a kite, a terrible hour or so as I zoned out, time lost and unaccounted for which was actually dangerous, anything could have happened. That stuff I believe was Damiana, don't burn it; these places sell allsorts of natural and legal stuff but one should only use if clued up, I wasn't.

So anyway, my fire pit had a massive grill for BBQing and the small BBQ/smoker was very handy; I had already read that burning some human parts does smell, you can't just like stick it in the oven and do a roast. The meat that went onto the BBQ and into the smoker were from particular areas with no fat. Lean meat only, which to be honest wasn't that much given the specimen's physiques.

Some bones can be put into direct heat, they then become dry and brittle and are easily pulverized. Skin is surprisingly easy to peel once one is dead, it is leathery and cold and easily separates from tissue; under the skin there's yellow fat which, when it contacts warmth, liquifies. Tendons and ligaments can't be slashed as such, they are protected by surrounding tissue and they slide out the way without being cut; you have to apply pressure with a sawing action, ripping motion, like when you cut a steak.

Nothing about it is easy, one needs time, space, effort, concentration and motivation of course.

I was also already aware that the best way to kill someone is by a sharp unexpected blow to the head, as any struggle for life, pumps a greater volume of blood and secretions throughout the body due to adrenaline; making the clearout and clear up messier.

It is priority to minimise the mess; remember first things first and begin with the end in mind. Focus, concentration, step by step, no cutting corners, excuse the pun.

WARNING:
GO TO PAGE 78
IF YOU DO NOT WANT TO READ
THE SHORT VERSION OF
DISMEMBERMENT & DECAPITATION
IT DEPENDS ON YOUR
HORROR STORY PREFERENCE

To begin one has to basically perforate the body with a sharp knife, this is like stabbing meat through when cooking, not like stabbing holes in the plastic of your microwave meal; this is actually time consuming and could be perceived as one enjoying stabbing that person but that's not quite the case. It's a necessary action to perform a function, there was nothing else behind that! When you smack a steak to make it tender you aren't consciously thinking you're beating a cow in some warped manner, although it is a good tension release.

To drain the blood (in the bath obviously) you have to block off the drain outlet first, you can't send approximately 6 litres of blood into the household drains and expect it to just go off on its merry way.

I just want to say at this point as it just popped into my head, how the devil gets hold of us all at some time in our lives; I had a mind pop of the dinner table on christmas day; it was upended over me, the boiling gravy scolded my legs, the entire turkey slid off along with all the trimmings, crockery, cutlery, glasses, lit candles and the heavy glass festive centrepiece. It was a terrible mess and the white wall behind me was a wash with many colours including red wine. That gravy had come out of the microwave bubbling as he had a thing about hot gravy, it scolded and it hurt a lot. The reason he did that was because, according to him, the turkey was dry. But only an idiot would believe that was the reason, it was because he was simply a nasty barsteward prone to bursts of violence.

One year when the kids were young he had a massive fit of temper, he ripped down the christmas tree in front of them then set light to the ceiling trimmings; they were the old fashion type silver and gold metallic ones. They melted and shrivelled and gave off loads of terrible smelling smoke; dangerous and a nasty action for the kids to witness.

Another year the tree went out before it was decorated, it had stabbed him in the eyeball whilst he was putting it up and he had to go to A&E. It must have been me talking about the bodies that bought this to mind as I guess one could say it's similar to skinning and dressing a turkey; and in saying how the devil gets hold of us sometimes, well, I wasn't being strictly truthful about stabbing to perforate the body, as if I'm going to be totally honest in writing all this, then yes, yes I did get satisfaction from perforating him, so there we are.

So, in draining the blood, one needs to put the bath plug in, perforate the body then with a very sharp knife which has a long handle, cut from ear to ear, making sure to cut through the neck and larynx, from one side to the other to sever the internal and external carotid arteries, being the major blood vessels that carry the blood from the heart to the brain.

Once that is done one has to perform CPR, you don't have to do it fast and in time on an already deceased body; the CPR action assists draining the body by pumping. Then cut the fronts of the thighs, deeply and diagonally to slit the femoral arteries then continue to pump the chest like CPR. After death the valves in the heart still work, the bounceback of the ribcage gives a sort of suction to the atria, similar to a plunger down a blocked drain one could say.

Then one has to decapitate; continue the cut of the throat from the jawline right to the back of the head. Slice the muscle and ligament then basically grip and twist the head, in which it comes right off. I had perfected this by the third time, it separates where the spinal cord meets the skull.

Once all the blood is drained, run the bath water with it when you unplug and also add a fair amount of bleach; the bleach deodorises the smell of death and avoids the stench coming back up the drains and gets rid of any clinging traces in the pipework.

As I didn't want the entire bodies bleached I had to keep them off the bathtub base, for this I used my dead mother's mobility aids, of which there were many bath ones; I found the seats that fit into the base of the bath easy to use during the entire process and the over-bath seat was very handy serving as a sort of instrument shelf.

I'm not sure why I kept them all to begin with, maybe in the back of my mind I thought I would need them myself one day. But anyway, they are all gone now, bleached, sterilised and given away to a charity who by now would have passed them on to be used as intended.

Dennis Nilsen made some mistakes with his drains but that wasn't just blood, he blocked the drains with body parts, I did not.

So anyway, the water needs to be run for a good twenty minutes with the bleach, it prevents sewer gases like the toilet u-bend does. No open windows and doors whilst doing all this of course, the best time to ventilate being after the fact, where I plugged in an ioniser and had bowls of baking soda and burnt the pagan fragranced stuff and used scented candles.

I'm sure that it is hard to imagine but you can cut a body into several pieces quicker than you think; but not as quick and easy as boning a chicken. When taking a break, which one has to of course as it takes time and effort, you need to cover the body and parts up with plastic sheeting for obvious reasons; the sheets burned up pretty quickly in the fire pit, an initial bit of dark smelly smoke but with all the other flammables and nice smells it wasn't too noticeable, a bit like when you put undried garden foliage on the fire and it smokes initially.

When all fluids are drained and the head is off, expose the bones by cutting through; that meat cleaver was of good use, I'm sure he is now glad that he bought that case back home. I had to obtain another saw bench and put it on the patio and periodically stand outside sawing wood, all of which ended up in the fire pit but no one knew that; the sawn wood was an added bonus as I was only sawing so that people thought I was doing DIY, which wasn't out of place.

I hammered, drilled, used the heat gun, dragged stuff, put stuff from the loft onto the fire, put free stuff out the front of the house, moved stuff around in the shed, ordered new things for delivery. I ordered wood and left it outfront on the drive, the noise was not out of the ordinary. I jet washed the patio, paths, sides of the house; rearranged the garden and looked like some other board person in lockdown amusing themselves, which I most certainly was; no one noticed.

Anyway, joints, a hammer and the meat cleave, big smacks to drive it through, it got easier with practice; **(the face shield finally came in handy)** cut through the armpit straight to the shoulder blade; chop the hands off about an inch above the wrist. I used the large thick meat chopping board that came from a sainsburys sale, excellent bargain, it was burnt in the end, I had no intentions of keeping it anyway, hefty item.

Cut into and break apart the elbow joint so that there's two parts to each arm; chop the feet off about 3 inches up from the ankle. Cut from the solar plexus, the point between the breast bone and the stomach, to almost the anus; the pubic bone requires sawing through.

Before pulling out all the innards which need cutting away from the back wall of the body (large and small intestines, kidneys, liver, stomach ect) one needs good quality, large freezer bags and have them open and ready.

The parts that can't be consumed by animals, can be stored in bags with bleach, in the freezer until it's safe to dispose of them. The consumables can't be in bleach otherwise the animals can't eat them, so they went directly into the freezer; the parts that went onto the BBQ and in the smoker were fine for the animals but not including offal.

Some parts I purposefully didn't make too much of a mess of, as on disposal they needed to be able to 'see' and 'hear' and 'feel'; therefore, 2 hearts and 2 heads were not mutilated, but the third I had to disfigure obviously.

Cut through the diaphragm, the muscular membrane dividing the upper and lower abdominal cavities; remove the breast bone, cutting down through each side where it connects to the rib then saw through and detach it from the collar bone. Cut the two halves into quarters by slicing through the side between ribcage and pelvis. The backbone is easily removed by cutting down either side of the tailbone directly through. Then chop to whatever length needed.

Saw through the legs directly below the groin and again a couple of inches above the knee. By skinning here the meat can be cut into steak like pieces and into fillets for animal consumption, which included the dogs, then dog. Oddly the cats wouldn't touch any but the fox was not fussy; a few times it even ate uncooked, small pieces it ate in situ, no large parts for it to carry off, I cut all small bits with scissors.

The meat cleaver served well on small bones, a hacksaw is also very useful but the serrated blades don't cut bones great, weighty blades break them. I used the food processor then gave it away; I hadn't overused it as clearly it would sound suspicious and it could have in fact ruined it.

There's a sewer drain in the garden for which I already had a set of drain rods (I wonder what else went down there over the years) it wasn't out of the ordinary to lift that lid. The new development had already caused an issue in the vicinity of 1 Narcissist Road; as predicted as they allowed the newbuilds on old 4 inch drains when it really required 6 inch. The house at the bottom of the hill needed a flood plate fitted on the drain in their garden as a few times it all came up in the garden when everything blocked up.
These developers cut corners and the local councils take backhanders; so it wasn't completely out of the ordinary to lift the drain cover and use the drain rods and to run the hosepipe down; this allowed me to get rid of small parts that the rats would get rid of as they weren't ever going to pop up in the garden down the hill, it has a fixed flood plate doesn't it.

As I've said, heated bones makes them dry and brittle so were really easy to smash up or blend to crumbs, but the bigger bones were not suitable for that.

Some parts needed to be incinerated, these went into the dog poo bins dotted all across the town; but I had to pick and choses bins by pretending to put poop in (it was grass I picked up) on the dog walks. If they were too full I couldn't, if they were empty I couldn't, they had to be half full in a fairly popular area, not out of the way where no one would put anything on top relatively quickly.

I don't know if you have dogs, but all us walkers know to stand well back when depositing as there are usually flies and the bins stink god awful, no one would be sticking their head over to peer in, a genius disposal place if i say so myself, straight to the incinerator.

With heads / skulls, once disposed of correctly, scavengers, ants, maggots consume, so they need to be secured so that a larger scavenger doesn't take it off and leave it to be found. Both heads in town are secured, the last one out of town is not so well secured to be honest but it is very unlikely it will be dragged off anywhere, deep inside there are densely overgrown dark areas with pits of yucky water and broken fallen trees, it is weighted, and I did dig it down and given the time span since, I'd say I'm safe on that. I could have done with waders at the time but it wasn't planned that far in advance and I didn't really know exactly what and where until I got there, I had a rough idea but not exact specifics.

All parts of the first two are in differing locations as it is not wise to return to the same site to dispose; the last is all in one area but different parts, like I said, it took me an entire day, but I did get lost; I've never gone back to dispose again.

I read so many articles of how people got caught that I think I was pretty clued up. I kept nothing, used one area of this house, got rid of most things that I used; I even sold all the Le Creuset as a large set which included my weapon of choice. I burnt, buried, gave away, used clothing banks all over the place, charity dumps. I cleaned, scrubbed and eliminated to the naked eye; however, a black light may tell a different story. No carpet or flooring has been replaced as taking them to recycle centres maybe a stupid mistake, likewise the butchers case is still in my possession. The house could do with burning down.

Getting caught is not in my plans, I need to see what living a free life is like., well as free as it can be under the New World Order.

Anyway, I was extremely methodical in order to be careful and I did nothing that would draw attention. Jeffery Dahmer got caught by him boiling body parts, the stench was apparently terrible; the green river killer excelled at disposal as he chose openly accessible areas that were too large to be patrolled much; conversely, Richard Crafts got caught from the finding of 2 teeth and some hair after putting his wife into the wood chipper.

There's a book, The ability to Kill, that has case studies of those that almost perpetrated the perfect murder but were caught on one stupid detail; and then there are all those that I worked with.

On a note, I didn't realise before how noisy plastic is, plastic in its many forms is the devil's invention, waterproof, leak proof yet annoying. It's noisey, in the quietness, plastic is really loud, how does something so thin make so much noise?
Even a salad bag more than rustles, it crackles and is actually loud, plastic sheeting, snap on lids, microwave meals plastic doesn't just

pop when pricked. The plastic that food comes in is like fortnox and to rid it is tricky; I ended up burning all plastic and that is really bad for the environment. (or so they say)

How did we ever get by pre plastic? Probably healthier but that's by the by, what I'm saying is, in the quietness plastic makes a noise, if it can't be seen, it can be heard. Using just cling film wouldn't suffice unfortunately, nevertheless, each disposal was in solitude, aside from the dogs / dog; clearly I wasn't seen or heard as I wouldn't be sitting here writing this.

So there you have it, not a step by step nor dismemberment for dummies and not at all a graphic account. I don't consider myself a crimal as for that label one has to commit a crime; the biggest difference between most criminals and other people is that the criminals became so as they were stupid enough to get caught; I did not. On a small note, in all the reading I did, I read something about stamped self addressed envelopes and how they were used to kill; the individuals licked the seal to close it but it was laced with poison and by the time the envelopes had gone back to whence they came, the individuals died after posting the evidence back to the sender. So there we are, never lick addressed stamped envelopes.

I expect you are thinking what type of person is able to dismember and dissect without batting an eyelid; my answer to that question can only relate to the type of person that I am, if at all I fall into a specific type. I want to be understood, it's one of the reasons that I'm writing this. I can only explain things from my subjective viewpoint, I cannot speak for anyone else, after all, we all have our own reasons of why we do what we do; some people fall neatly into a label in which all their traits fit, whether by birth and biology or by environment.

I don't believe I fit into any specific category, as I've said before, I didn't and don't think the same as my family, I never did.

I've never gone out of my way to cause harm to anyone, I've only ever reacted. I have no desire to be the best at anything, in fact I'm not particularly good at anything apart from blending into backgrounds and being inconspicuous, like I've said, I'm a nobody, forgotten, invisible.

There was never a conscious plan for that first time, despite wanting to harm and ruin him over the years, he was such an arrogant, argumentative, temper throwing bully that he pretty much ruined himself. Walked from every job, not able to go into any pub, fell out with any friends he ever made; his path of destruction couldn't be rebuilt; he destroyed himself, self sabotage, without any help from me. Maybe I got satisfaction from that, I hadn't planned to end his life, it was just the opportunity in a perfect moment in time.

After the fact, I had to deal with all the consequences of my actions, it wasn't a difficult choice, deal with it or go to prison for the rest of my life, meaning I would have been imprisoned one way or another my entire life span.

Obviously anyone with an ounce of sense and a will to survive and live freely would choose to simply deal with it, so I did. The second time was not planned either and one could say the second was a consequence of the first. Once those two were done and dusted I honestly thought it was the end of it all. From then on the plan was to obtain extra funds, look 'normal', wait out the pandemic restrictions and leave; the third and last was nothing to do with the first or second, it was an entirely different entity, it was a separate pretty much unrelated happening.

I could say that the end result was premeditated whereupon to have allowed that beast to continue to roam would have been irresponsible after knowing what he was.

If he had of continued to be in society someone somewhere would have fallen foul of his encounter, it would have been like I withheld vital information and the consequences of that meant harm came to another; but neither could I draw attention to these walls, 1 narcissist road would have been pulled apart and into the public eye, I couldn't allow that to happen.

I was caught between a rock and a hard place, I made the right choice based on the risk assessment and had the necessary skills to get out of that predicament and I learnt from it.

The type of person that I am isn't from the dark triad, I don't have unpleasant personality traits, I hope that you understand that. In times of crisis you do what you have to do, that's how you deal with it, it's only a problem if you perceive it to be; so you have to be methodical and I guess have an element of detachment, but I didn't feel detached, it was more of a controlled concentration. The last one I had no thought on at all, I didn't even think about what he may possibly have done in the past and what he may possibly have done in the future, it was simply something I had to do, I took no enjoyment, just relief when the task was complete.

Like I've already said, I did get some satisfaction from perforating the first, probably years of wanting to revenge for his nasty acts upon the kids, so stabbing his body may be perceived as sick and twisted to those that have never been on the receiving end of cruelty; cutting him up was neither here nor there aside from stapling his eyelids open and bagging his heart of stone, everything else was just a task, but those hands won't ever slap anyone in the face again that's for sure.

With the second I probably chose to not think too deeply and just remember the adult it had become; of course his behaviour toward her aided the development but it was born of the devil and I'm pretty sure, had it of grown up elsewhere and not narcissist road, it would still have developed into some similar form of what it did due to biology.

So, to sum up, what type of person depends on the situation; can you yourself categorically say that you could never do such a thing? Even if your life depended on it?

If someone had asked me that question a few years back I would have said don't be ridiculous, leave that to the crazies.

But let me tell you, all three belonged to the dark triad, so it's no loss. In case you aren't familiar with the dark triad, it represents the 3 unpleasant personality traits, of which you will be aware of, 'narcissism' of which I've already talked about, 'psychopathy' and 'machiavellianism'.

All 3 traits are about putting oneself first and getting what you want. A combination of all 3 traits makes for a danger to others mental wellbeing; it becomes overwhelming and it causes great mental distress and damage to have such a person in your life.

Imagine if you will, an entire family let alone one individual, like I said, I've got nerves of steel and I don't think the same, but you end up doubting your own instincts and end up co-depending (addiction) to having them in your life; the only way out, being to extricate them from your life for good, by taking that quantum leap or else the parting will only occur by death, be it normal causes or otherwise.

These 'types' of people are difficult to be around, there is a lack of family commitment unless it's a wrong doing, then it becomes a matter of the family being committed to keeping it within the family by coercion and or abuse.

Why are those traits deemed as dark? Because of their malevolent qualities, malevolent being the deliberateness to cause harm.

All three traits overlap and are associated with callous, manipulative behaviour, persistent in narcissist road. These personalities compete rather than cooperate with you; they can be spiteful, hostile, vicious and malicious.

They are never satisfied and dislike the truth that contradicts their thinking, they do not appreciate being told what to do and work environments are tricky; the preference being environments where rules are ambiguous, where basically they perform better as they can do what they want.

I was the only person in the family, including the marriage, that stayed working in a profession that involved strict rules and regulations, and even after leaving that years later, I then went into agency work and worked in hundreds of different establishments in which, being an agency worker, most times I was at the mercy of being given instructions of what to do and when; I performed extremely well. I think differently, I am not selfish or manipulative, I take it but rarely dish it, I'm not competitive nor disagreeable and being unagreeable is the strongest sign that correlates with the dark triad.

Like I've said, my dad and his family (but not his mum) were always right even when they were wrong. The dark triad really was a dark place to live when you don't belong to it; you become submissive to many a bad deed, it's normal but you become aware it's abnormal, you are part of it as you're living it, but you aren't like it.

As a child I had no choice, as an adult I was a conscious cooperator and all these people made me who I am today; on the other hand I allowed it, I co-created.

All but two from 1 narcissist road displayed traits from the dark side, some more so than others but violence was the common denominator mainly in the males.

Some gained pleasure in watching negative events unfold, but not all. There was such a mish mash of bad behaviours that it would be difficult to label an individual with a stand alone personality trait but narcissism was the main identifiable one, shared by all bar two.

Machiavellianism is mainly about manipulation, I consider this trait joined my m-field by marriage and explains the genetic inheritance to that offspring (his daughter). I think this is the worst of the dark triad, they prey and hunt and if their intelligence isn't enough and they lack particular skills, their frustration leads to violence, bursts of violent temper rages.

Having lived with this, my theory is that they are aware they lack particular skills to make it to the big time, but that's where they really want to be, no matter how much effort they've put in, despite coming across as charming, confident and clever, they can't quite cut the mustard and the display of the peacock's tail eventually shows it is in fact a turkey; the knock back causes outrage and violence commences.

Some however do possess the skills and intelligence and here the violence is less, they don't need to be violent as they aren't frustrated, they're achieving their goals.

Let me make this a bit clearer from my personal observations; the now in eternal purgatory spouse's father was a typical machiavellian with high intelligence. If he hadn't of been inflicted with the dark side he would have gone far professionally.

To sum up the trait, they are only focused on their own well-being, they are cunning, come across as charming and smart, they are patient and calculating, manipulative, self interested with an absence of morality. They exploit for self gain, use flattery, lie and deceive, cheat, steal, lack values, unempathetic; sometimes aloof and not always calculate the consequences of their actions.

They scheme, prey and hunt down, use, chew up and spit out. They are untrustworthy and consequently they trust no one.

They can be cynical and they have power over relationships and are capable of causing harm; there is inauthenticity of perceived good actions, they make good con artists, they only become criminals when they're caught.

His father was intelligent, he was not, he wasn't illiterate, but his brain lacked savvy cells and he didn't have the looks whereas his father did. So let me give you a brief rundown of that m-field. It isn't my family, not my blood, I joined it's m-field by marriage for far too many years, but I'm not writing about that family in detail, only about how it came to influence my life and my m-field.

So in brief, the father was born in a city to a low income family with many siblings, he was the youngest. If I cannot say with certainty that something is a fact, I can only say it's hearsay; so hearsay says that it was a small terraced abode, inner city, not an affluent area and was usual to be overcrowded; of those siblings, all the males turned to crime, some being involved in notorious gangs of that time. The father being the youngest, did not get caught for any crime and married young.

Stapled eyelids was the first born. The father (hearsay says) was a womaniser and also now a criminal (caught for crime) during those early years of marriage, mean to his wife (the mother) cruel to his offspring (hearsay) and would smash up toys and bikes and house objects etc. Hearsay also says that one of the brothers got so angry after punching the chimney breast and hurting his hand that he then bit a chunk out of the chimney breast. I add this hearsay just to give an example of the ludicrous talk in boasting about that family; it is obvious that unless the chimney breast was made of cake, one would only break one's teeth on the brick.

Anyway, the couple split up due to the behaviour of the father, the mother could do nothing with that first born, he ran away frequently, including out of school, had temper fits and rages, destroyed things and was apparently more than difficult. He wanted to be with his father, so the mother took him and left him there, fulfilling his wish. He grew up blaming his mother for the subsequent nomadic life he led with various lady friends of his father's, in various locations including being on the run (hearsay) but he could have gone back to his mother any time; he demonised her, she was the villain, he was the victim. He was forever the victim, nothing was ever his fault, the sob story being, he was a dumped infant who led an awful childhood and everything that he did thereafter was due to this; plans not realised were due to his victim status. Hearsay says he witnessed crimes, cons, violence, threats and being on the run without food or clothing.

I will admit, initially I fell for this victim sob story but particular things didn't add up and as time went on he became more and more abusive and controlling, but that's not what I'm talking about here. Some years into our marriage, the father appeared for a brief time, driving flash cars (this is where I saw the first car phone).

When the father saw his son disrespect his wife (me) he actually gave him a beating in the hallway and gave him a lecture on abuse toward females. It was then that I realised that his behaviour of physical violence was not learnt from his father (which I thought it was) but he had not behaved that way, he didn't need to. The father then disappeared for a few years; when contact was made again, he was then in prison. No flash cars for a while; but to cut a long story short he got caught a few more times, timeshares abroad, conning lonely older females out of their homes and money, then a rather big con that hit the newspapers and crimewatch (I kid you not) of which I cannot tell you about here obviously.

Drama drama drama, showmanship, competitiveness, boastfulness, win, lose, have, have not, manipulating, scheming, lying, cheating but ultimately all failures in a destructive m-field where cutting the mustard meant committing offences and hurting people just to have some moments of living a high life; repeatedly changing your name, ripping off your own family and spitting on everyone you ever meet. How exhausting that must have been to live it, but I guess he had the energy as only death in old age stopped him.

The truth of it all is that the merging of our two families m-fields resulted in chaos and dangerous dysfunction; I bought it to an end that day. It took me well over 30 years to end that co-existence and over 50 years to sever the umbilical cord from the walls to which I was born.

Was this a conscious thought over time? No, no it wasn't.

I had not given the thought of leaving any consideration in 40 years; the one time I did escape was when I was 15, I was bought back by the authorities and had to attend court for not going to school.

I had gone away for the summer and simply refused to return.

SUMMER OF FREEDOM:

Let me briefly explain:

We were on our usual annual holiday for a week, the same place, the same week, the same caravan site every year due to the races, my fathers choice. Some years we went with the extended family, some with the grandparents, some not.

This particular week it was the not; the family in the caravan next door mixed a bit with us, to cut a long story short, that summer I was invited to stay with them to look after the youngest child while the mother was at work.

Don't you find that somewhat strange that my mother partook in this?

Why on earth did she do that?

I was 15, granted I was streetwise and able to defend myself but she let me go to a family she hardly knew to a house in a city that she'd never been to.

Was it her way or belief that she was setting me free?

What she didn't know, I'm sure, is that they were a bunch of dysfunctional drinkers, however, they were never mean to me.

I had no knowledge of inner city activities of the youth, I came from a market town. I had expert knowledge in abuse, cruelty and suicide attempts, but none in drugs and glue sniffing.

My introduction to city life for the working class wasn't what I was expecting. I spent the summer in and around a run down estate, closed factories, abandoned buildings, looking at incarcerated individuals through the fence of the 'mental institution', jumping canals, running when the kids stole from the shops, being sold alcohol and glue sniffing! Nice huh?

My mum even sent the family allowance book pre-signed so that the mother there could cash it to feed me. It was one meal a night but plenty of cigarettes.

There was a club on the estate that served alcohol to literally anyone, the culture there was to go to work, come home, slap a meal together or not, there was always the chippy, then go to the club whilst the offspring ran amok; however, there was no brutality, no kids getting beatings nor wives come to that. Unruly yes, hostile no.

I wasn't completely happy staying there, it felt like some weird holiday camp where kids fend for themselves, the adults were present but it didn't feel like adult.

The positive being that nothing horrible happened there, no violence, no walking on eggshells.

However, bad habits were gained and too much freedom led to irresponsible behaviour.

When it was time to return I didn't want to go, that decision was supported by that family of whom I had not confided in, the last thing I would ever do was shame myself let alone the family; they supported me for reasons unbeknown to me.

My mum sent letters as neither was on the phone, so did the local authority, then there was a visit and I was returned home.

On return I had to go to court and was sent to a school for delinquents three days a week. Times have changed since then but back then if you were lucky you got the school referral for 6 months, if not it was the 'boarding school'; if you didn't attend the day school you would be taken and sent to the boarding one. Considering I already was aware of my dad's time in borstal, there was no way I would have skipped the day school after court.

I didn't even think that my not returning when I should have would have resulted in court, I was 15 you could leave at 16, but it happened anyway. My dad was furious, my mum was not; he was of the opinion that I'd been given an inch and had taken a yard. I wasn't afraid of any consequences at home at the time, I wasn't there was I; it was a bit like saying if I close my eyes you can't see me since I can't see you.

Immaturity got in the way of rational thought, of course there would be consequences, making the parents look bad; but to the outside world I had gone away for the summer, liked the freedom, got a bit delinquent and was pulled back in line.

The day school for delinquents turned out to be a blast; we didn't do any work, it was frequented by social workers and psychologists, the unwritten rule of such places was, you said nothing, laughed off prying questions, attended every day that you were meant to, it was over in 6 months.

The day of the court I wore a dress, not ordinary for me, blond curly hair hanging down, minded my manners, admitted to not wanting to come back as I was having too much fun, said sorry even though I wasn't, it was over quickly.

I never thought about the future really, but I was a kid, why would I. But now all these years on I do wish I had a wayback machine; where did the years go. It's true when they say that life is but the blink of an eye. Aside from that one weird summer the rest of my life 'thus far' had been the usual endless round of living on a knife edge; who'd have thought I'd end up using the knife edge.

There's an old saying, 'the body can't go where the mind hasn't been'; an interesting saying don't you think. I first heard that in 1995 from a driving instructor, it's stuck in my head ever since. I assumed it meant, if you want to do something and don't know how, you need to learn and think about it before you embark, whereupon mind and body will be on the same page.

So I found myself wondering if I had ever envisaged smacking him in the face with an extremely heavy object, as I did so with such ease and precision without standing there thinking about it first, like it was second nature and as though I had done it before.
Had I been there before in my mind?

Of course I'd not dismembered before, the mind had never been there for sure as I was pretty clueless, of that I did have to inform the mind before anyone's body did anything.
So there may lay the difference, possibly, that a task which requires longer concentration requires conscious attention whereas an involuntary response or action is via the subconscious, which doesn't involve long concentration, whereby your mind knows what it's doing even though you do not. Just a thought!
But how does consciousness work anyway?
We are basically just a bunch of cells and when you see the body all cut up and see parts in person (so to speak) you have to stop and wonder how this all works as a walking, thinking machine, how did that all come about?

It's no wonder there are many mistakes in the making, it's complex. The thinking part, the brain, is a complex organ in itself, almost 100 billion neurons, each connected to 10 thousand others, something like 10 trillion nerve connections.

This jelly lump of tissue expresses who we are, it's a marvel no? How does this have a conscious and unconscious that cannot be seen, they aren't observable, invisible even to science.

It isn't like I could have looked at their brains and pinpointed the neurons labelled dark triad or the manipulator neurons or the cruel neurons.

Consciousness means we are aware, aware of what we are thinking, feeling, doing and why. So people are fully aware when they are being cruel or nasty or nice.

The unobservable nature of consciousness can only be seen by the expression of behaviour, but if you ask someone a question they can easily lie, for all tense and purpose you wouldn't know as you can't see what they are thinking; well not yet anyway but they have already begun to experiment with brain chips (Human Augmentation).

So maybe one day in the not so distant future the conscious will be shown and they may even find the unconscious and tell you what that's thinking, before it communicates with you.

When they do achieve that, the human body will be part AI (Artificial Intelligence) and we will be so controlled and programmed that consciousness and unconsciousness won't matter, they will be bypassed anyway.

Have a look on your government website to view the papers on human augmentation.

All humans will become predictable, all bad behaviours ceased, all unhealthy habits eradicated, no cruelty, no crime.

Efficient and effective brains without spontaneity or the ability to do harm.

You may think that is all sci fi and many years in the future, but you are wrong, it's coming. Experiments are already happening with animal brains and I wouldn't be the least surprised if they've already implanted in the heads of untreatables and somewhere in the world, newborn babies.

Every discovery we know today began somewhere didn't it, only disclosed to us when all unethical happenings are hidden; they didn't wake up one morning with the knowledge, only after many experiments, observations and follow-ups.

Although they know a lot about the brain, they've yet to capture the way the brain gives us the aware and unaware / conscious and unconscious (the smart part).

Was my dad consciously aware when he lashed out on being woken? No, I don't believe so; I believe that it was an ingrained self defence mechanism, not from his home life as he was gone from that before he was 13, that particular behaviour developed through borstal.

On leaving Borstal it was straight into national service; he never spoke about his years at home but he hated a particular older brother, he never said why. As for borstal, the only reference he ever made was to make us sit and watch 'Scum' when it came on the TV. His forced action in not giving us a choice of leaving the room effectively told his story.

So his involuntary actions on being woken, you could understand. Like I've said, if he had been to the pub and you woke him then rage would follow the initial unconscious response; of this I am not sure if he had control or not, was it blind rage?

Did he know that he was punching and kicking his child at the time, but the rage had to come out?

Or was he seeing his past abusers?

No one will ever know, he never said, we never asked, he nor anyone else ever spoke about these frequent happenings, they were normality.

Because they were frequent occurrences one doesn't dwell on every event, only particular episodes imprint on one's brain. Of these one tries to keep them locked away, which means if they resurface it's hard to push them back in and keep them there. The images that are ingrained aren't the actions of the brutality, it's the images of the faces of those during the event.

It is hard to describe what fear and pain looks like on a face; you can see the fear and see the pain but how to describe it here is beyond my writing capabilities. It isn't a sad face with tears, imagine a face contorted with each blow, eyes wide open in fear when the fist is raised, shut tight and mouth wide open on impact; a face pleading as the body is being dragged by the hair from the room where it knows what's about to be received.

One hand clutched to the hand pulling the hair, the other hand searching for something to grab onto as you're dragged along the floor, the desperate attempt to stop what is about to commence.

The face of someone trying to fend off the whipping of the wire clothes hanger, each connecting whip contorts the face of which I find it hard to describe, the pleading, the begging, to stop.

The face responding to the buckle end of the belt repeatedly lashing the back, the legs and the arms used in defence; to describe fear and pain in a face doesn't suffice, until you see it, you cannot understand.

My older male sibling boar the brunt of my dad's rages, unconscious and conscious, because he was relatively stupid. In this day and age he would possibly be diagnosed autistic or with some type of brain damage, my mother said it was a long and difficult birth; he had no social skills, he didn't know when to shut up and misread boundaries. I didn't have much to do with him in the growing up years, I had my younger male sibling and the various cousins that came and went; to me he was stupid but of course back then it was a simple case of taking care of yourself.

There was relief that it wasn't you this time, like I said, one learnt to not care deeply but those images imprinted on my brain nonetheless, as no doubt my brain was traumatised by the events and the human cruelty.

My dad was generous with his money, we wanted for little, but he was too generous with his brutality. One didn't back chat, the sober conscious discipline he dished out was not always a prolonged sustained attack, it was short and sharp but just as painful.

One time my mum whinged to my dad when he came in that my younger brother was still in bed, to this day I've no idea why my mother would dob us in to our dad knowing full well what he would do. Anyway, it was a Saturday, my dad went up the stairs, into the bedroom, grabbed my brother by the hair whilst he was asleep and unprepared, he dragged him out the bed and down the stairs backwards like a caveman dragging a kill; he dragged him into the lounge and beat him in front of my mother then said, he's up now; sat on the couch and watched TV.

My mother sat in the armchair, she didn't move a muscle nor speak, my brother was crying in a ball on the floor.

I remember standing there not knowing whether to move or not, my instinct was to help my brother, my instinct was to not move a muscle; I hope that makes sense, but the instinct to help my brother overruled my instinct to not move a muscle, or it was stubbornness, who knows, but on bending down to reach out, I saw the movement out the side of my eye and it was too late; cause and effect, I knew better than that, the consequences were mine to suck up.

Another time in my early teens, again a Saturday, my mother had left a note and a list, not uncommon, she worked so we were used to getting stuff. The note read 'Dart Flights', that is what it looked like. Considering my dad was a dart player and we had dart boards and darts all over the house, and my dad was in a few teams and had trophies, it didn't seem wrong in reading it.
I'd been before to that sports shop, with mum, to buy his flights. So, that is exactly what I did. I left them in the lounge on his side table, with the change, then went out to mess about with the usual crowd. Saturday afternoons our local shop was shut until Monday; there weren't the supermarkets of today.
Saturdays, shift depending, my dad would go to the pub. When I got home that evening I walked into the lounge and very unexpectedly was jumped by my dad; he came off the couch like he had a spring up his backside, it was that fast, a nanosecond, no time to run or get out the way.
He beat me quite badly that day and broke my nose, the beating was that bad that my older stupid sibling ran to the phone box and called the police. When the police came my dad ordered them off the property, they went and stood out behind the gate on the path. I was frog marched by my dad to the fence, they shone a torch on me, decided I was standing and not dieing and left.

The stupid sibling paid for his actions, reconfirming to me, that no good deed goes unpunished. It transpired that my mum had in fact written 'Dark Tights' which wasn't uncommon either; I had simply misread but she hadn't noticed the dart flights on dad's table, she assumed I had not bothered and complained to my dad who had been drinking, why? I still cannot understand why she did that, welcome to 1 Narcissist Road!

Just so you know, my offspring were not subjected to this type of brutality, they witnessed more than they physically experienced, but they were subjected to a different type of cruelty and mental abuse; for this I am deeply regretful of not killing him years ago. But of course I couldn't back then, there wasn't a pandemic and the offspring were there along with quite a few family members, but I should have got up and taken them away, but to where I'm not sure, it was all very different back then, not even many social security benefits existed; never mind the fact it would have meant leaving my home and family; hindsight is as they say, a wonderful thing.

By their time things had changed a bit and there was the introduction of the Children's Act, a few other policies meant there were some state powers and a few prying eyes, but clearly things weren't as they are today; back then most interventions were still perceived as an intrusion on family life and domestic violence was still pretty much ignored by the police; it has taken many many years for progress in such areas of family life. But like I've said, the rules were the rules, family matters were just that.
But I will say, I am not excusing myself.

My offspring grew up with the same rules and were also aware of the presence of my fathers hold and the rules of this house and family; they were in the mold but it had changed shape. With each death the m-field shifted, but with each death the predominant dark traits from outside the family got bigger and meaner; it spread like bacteria in perfect conditions and eventually dominated.

Life went from one ruler to another but the latter was mentally crueler, abuse was premeditated and bare face lies took over; unpredictable behaviours and baffling occurrences.

One could say that previously one knew where one stood and there appeared to be reasons for most events, but that disappeared with deaths and one ended up living an unpredictable existence, a different type of cruelty, same walls, different evil. Like I've said, I'm not excusing myself, I allowed this to continue. I co-created the environment that those kids grew up in, I co-created as I allowed it; merely protesting but not taking action is inexcusable, it doesn't cut the mustard. I was not timid nor brow beaten, I wasn't shaking in my shoes, I wasn't bothered by his violence. A 'normal' person would have been but I'm not normal am I.

Just like all the other mother's in this family, I didn't take my responsibilities to where they should have been; that very first punch in the stomach whilst I was pregnant should have been the last, it could have ended there and then and I wouldn't be sitting here today writing this. Maybe I would have spent the years unattached, whatever, but I'm sure I wouldn't have wasted them and neither would I be in this position that I am today.

Since I did what I did I've asked myself why I lived that life; now that I am not in it, I look at it differently and wonder who exactly that person was, as that is not who I am now and wasn't before I met him, how many of me are there exactly?

WARNING VIOLENCE:

I sometimes wish that he had been more aware after I smashed him in the face and that I had taken more time in the kill; that he was paralysed but aware, so that I could do some of the things to him that he had done to others, that would have been a proper eye for an eye wouldn't it.

I could have broken his shin by kicking it with steel toe cap boots, I could have jumped on his stomach, done a viscous knee drop on his chest, backhanded him in his mouth whilst wearing a ring and split his mouth open, side kicked him in his stomach, punched his face, kicked him in the back, cracked him in the face with my knee, strangled him, smothered him with a cushion whilst kneeling on his chest, pushed my hands over his mouth and nose and pressed down really hard, smashed the remote control in his face, bent his fingers back until he screamed, put his arms behind his back and pushed them up really hard as far as they would go; bear hugged him from behind until all his breath had left and he thought he was going to die (he did that to the kids), pushed him on the floor and stood on his back, swung him around by his hair, elbowed him in the face whilst driving (not possible as he would have been immobilised) but elbowed him in the face nonetheless; punched his head and slapped his face a hundred times; then chucked hot coffee in his face, followed by hot meals attached to plates; but as stated, **hindsight is a wonderful thing isn't it, as I didn't do any of the above since the first blow probably killed him;** the second and third were to ensure and for luck.

I'm a bit annoyed that I didn't think about it all first, as now **he will never know what any of what he did to others actually feels like,** but I can only hope that the little people come for all abusers of children.

I will never know for sure but I did my best to have him suffer in the afterlife. It's a shame he was already dead when I stapled his eyelids, had he been alive I may have been compelled to have used the staple gun on his eyeballs as well and grated his face with the cheese grater; put his hands in the blender, stapled his mouth shut whilst I did it so no one heard him scream; but that's all pretty sick and twisted and just vengeful wishful thinking.

Instead he is doomed to the inbetween of the afterlife drowning in dirty beer, eaten, walked on, burned and crushed.

They say that violence breeds violence but I don't think that's strictly true; he was violent but hadn't experienced violence upon himself; I didn't express violence (unless in defence) despite experiencing it upon myself. But having said that, the males of my father's family were all violent. So one can't say for sure the reasons why unless there are differing reasons; If it's learnt behaviour, in the genes or being violent to control, or that you are simply a nasty person, or uncontrolled anger or mental instability.

Regardless of the reasons, unless you are mentally deranged, one would realise that it is not acceptable behaviour, unless of course you are dark triad material, in which case you just simply dont care. Like I've said, I'm not dark triad, neither was my younger sibling, can't speak for the elder, he was stupid and strange from birth; eventually got into trouble for not understanding boundaries, went from one failed relationship to another, got sectioned, put on psychiatric medication, unintentionally killed himself by mixing them with too much alcohol. But that's by the by, it was years ago.

The younger one lasted a bit longer, went off travelling, saw a lot of the world but in the states he caught a virus and back then it was relatively new and not treated as it is today; he died with help after a slow torturous decline. He never married, he lived his life on purpose as an adult, he didn't come back much after leaving but did send postcards from every country and when he did visit he would bring many gifts. He didn't have lasting relationships, he kind of blew around in the wind, he said he wasn't able to tolerate living with anyone. Unlike me, at least he left and actually lived a free life and escaped the death duties in the family.

They didn't all die off elderly, some went earlier; a cousin hung himself and we think we know why, another was killed in a fluke accident, and we had accidental suicides! But most of the rest was the usual; disease, cancer, heart issues, lung issues, but until now, no murders.
But do they count as family? Probably not, different genes, so no, none of the family were murdered.

There was one small potential attempt, when I was a child; whilst making my dad a cup of tea, I put rat poison in it from the cupboard under the sink but the tea turned green so I chucked it down the drain; just as well it did, I thought better of it after anyway.
I'm not sure if I would have actually given him it if it had not turned green, I will never know. I know I was very upset at the time, it was due to the singing ringing tree. I wonder how many of you know what that is; I hated it, I was petrified of that program and my dad forced me to watch it, every episode. I cried every time and he would give me something to cry for as crying at a tv program was apparently ridiculous and I should grow up. I don't wish to talk much about that program and that evil little being, you can look it up yourself.

My fear of it was a family joke and of much torment, carried on into later life even. Anyway, I didn't revenge with the rat poison, but had I continued it would have been intentional, although I'm sure I was unaware of the consequences at that age.

There's a singing ringing tree here in town, the first time I saw it was before any of what happened happened, it was relatively young at the time, I couldn't understand why it was there. They built a new development the other side of town, there's a field with a walk-through path connecting the development with a bridge to town. The tree looks random and out of place, one solitary tree in an otherwise barren field, it's growing on a sunken mound and it is the evil singing ringing tree. I was walking my dogs and hadn't been up that way in years; on seeing it I was stunned into stillness as I was taken back in my head.

I don't think it was intentionally planted there, it's out of place and I think it has grown like some evil panopticon observing the town below. I only went back there once, a few years on, with one dog, to offer it the heart of a dark triad, her's.
My belief is she will get back what she dished out; the singing ringing tree represents the stuff of all terror as a child, if you know of this program my guess is you've suppressed the memory.

Please accept my apologies for bringing this up and possibly unleashing terror into your brain. If you know to what I'm referring, then you, like myself whilst writing this, have shivers down your spine and a cold sweat bought on by anxious fear; that program was enough to fear paralyse any thinking child.

I'm very sorry if I have released the suppressed traumatic memory. I blame the government myself as the series was to broaden our worldly knowledge, 'Tales from Europe'.

Anyway the presumed moral of the warped program was that if you aren't a good person and aren't nice to people then something horrible will happen to you; the spiteful scheming personalities of the singing ringing tree is a more than meaningful disposal place for such a heart.

This evil panopticon surveys the town and looks down on two steeples, separated by speed, where one would expect to smell candyfloss, given the vicinity, but when the wind blows it's more like that of fermentation.

That night was so silent and I was uneasy; not of being seen as no one would walk there without a light, I would see them coming and my dog would hear them.

Digging a hole deep enough took more than a few minutes, I was digging in the dark, saving the top bit with grass on it.

I was on edge, my mind had gone back to that era of time and I was half expecting that evil dwarf to pop out from behind the tree; I had the jitters, the spooks.

When I'd done I walked on the area several times, it then dawned on me that I was walking on her heart, just the same as I had his.

Then I tied a plattered piece of her hair to a branch.

Why? Because it was some sort of warped peace offering to the evil tree, to keep the dark triad within its confines; some sort of sacrifice to the tree representing all evil in my life.

I don't even know if it is still there. It wasn't big of course, a small platt, a token of secured confinement whilst I walked away.

Given the months that have passed I'd say it probably blew away in the wind but I'm not going back to check, I've no wish to ever get close to that tree again.

I'm now closing the door on that memory for good, goodbye SRT.

Disposing of her head was a bit tricky, such a pretty face that I didn't want to spoil it. The looks of perfection were so deceiving however; what a waste, but there we are, she only ever used her looks to harm and trap, behind the pretty picture lay a bottomless pit of malevolence. But still, the face was a work of art. I did my best with makeup but I'd never been one for bothering. When young I got away with being naturally pleasant looking, but I didn't see this as an asset, such things can draw the wrong kind of attention as a child. What I'm saying is, I never bothered with makeup much anyway and when I did it wasn't the whole works, so trying to put makeup on her was not artistically done.

I just thought that the face deserved to be presented well on disposal.

What happened after the fact is obvious and the face would probably not get to decay. Nevertheless, presentation had been important in life, so I respected that in death.

Like I said, it wasn't something I had planned nor ever thought of occurring but I had no choice, I know she would have chucked me under the bus, and her return couldn't have been more unexpected than if it had of tried.

But, like I've also said, she can't ruin anyone else's life now can she, just like he can't since becoming the victim he always claimed to be.

It took several walks to choose the place specifically for a pretty face, deep in the ground or in water felt wrong. It was a strange find that day and where I was I wasn't consciously looking (maybe the subconscious was) I'd not noticed it before, the wind blew the leaves and there it was, I actually laughed out loud as the bars were so fitting, considering she jumped country before going to jail.

I stepped down without a thought to find the ditch was actually deeper, the floor was a mush of leaves and foliage blown in from the fields and the grill was actually bigger than that seen as exposed from above. I had to clear the foliage to see if the grill was fixed forever. I stood and pondered why there was even a grill; realised it was due to the foliage blowing down there and it being an issue with the drain. It wasn't a river ditch, I was standing in fields but the land slopes; there was also a concreted pathway which I presumed was access for farm machinery; the ditch is obviously for the rain water running off the land.
To where the water went I've no idea, the drain disappears under the land. On inspection the grill slid up and down, behind was just darkness. I tried to pull the grill up but it didn't move, there was nothing holding it except time.
I returned the next day (another long walk) with a can of spray lubricant, sprayed it all, tried to lift the grill but it only slightly gave, but it wouldn't slide up. So I sprayed it all again, pushed the leaves back and left.
Two days later I returned but I walked the route backwards; sprayed it again, pulled hard and up it came but only half way. I figured that her head would go in sideways, not upright; I shone the torch, it was just a drain to which I could not see the back of and only leaves that had gotten through the grill. I pushed it back down, sprayed it again, covered it and left.

I waited 3 days, then went back in the evening, her head in the backpack and the extending grabber that my mum used to use. We walked across the fields, part of the way of the king, then along the track, next to the black barn, at the foot of the large tree that threatens the neglected barn.

It was getting dark but I couldn't use the torch as a light shining here would have been seen and I'm sure would have been suspicious if not moving.

I hoped the grill would budge still, it did, but again only half way.

I had to get down on my hands and knees and be swift, as a silent, though unlikely passerby could look down on me.

I slid her head in sideways carefully, reached through and tried to stand it upright, it fell, I tried again, resting her on the side of the drain then slowly pushed it further back into the drain with the extending grabber.

Probably by falling over the makeup attempt got ruined but the grill wouldn't go up any further. I layed down and briefly shone the torch into the drain, from way back a pretty face of perfection looked back at me.

I shut the grill, pushed all the stuff back in front of it, walked away knowing nothing could take her off.

I continued on the dog walk so that he had an uninterrupted, at ease stroll.

I remember thinking as I walked away from her for the last time; everyone should pay their dues for their wrongs, what made these people think they were so different?

I wonder if she ever knew that her father's disdain for her was his belief that she was just like his father.

But I wonder also, if he was envious of them both in that their looks and capabilities far outstretched his. A strange observation and totally irrelevant now.

Dog walking is extremely good exercise plus it serves as relaxation if stressed, a slow plod if you just want to chill, a brisk intentional speedy pace releases tension and of course if you are hurried to leave an area; no matter the pace, no other looks with suspicion upon a dog walker. Neither does it appear out of place to emerge from overgrown areas, muddy fields, woods, forests, rivers, ditches, old overgrown cemeteries, day or night.

No dog walker was stopped and questioned in lockdown, it is obvious what one was doing; who would ask the stupid question 'what are you doing'? Walking the dog!
It didn't warrant a question, so no dog walker was asked, obviously. But at night I didn't actually see that many, the roads were empty as were the woods, footpaths along the riverbanks, bramble areas of the heath; there was plenty of wildlife and more than I'd noticed before or maybe I'd not noticed back then, when I was a different person, in a different life.

What I did see however, at the back of a particular hotel that backs onto a river, the car park was being used for exchanges of cash for illegal substances. I watched from my unobserved vantage point whilst feeding the rats, yes rats not cats.

I can see why they chose that area, the footpaths leading to it are accessible without going near a road and I not once have seen any law enforcer walking down there ever.
There are 5 ways to get there without road, 5 footpaths and 3 are not lit at night. The area is never busy at night anyway, but in lockdown it was deserted aside from the very few who didn't wish to be seen, myself included.

No one had any reason to go to the dead end where I went, there's no way out unless you wish to swim the river as the bridge is closed at night, the season dictates its closing time.

There are so many rats here that I've even seen them in the day crossing the bridge and not in lockdown, so imagine the presence with far less people about.

I don't know if you've ever seen rats drag food off, but they can carry a large amount by dragging and can drag about a pound in weight and they aren't fussy eaters either; but it was here that I discovered that ducks eat meat. I had no idea they did that and was a bit concerned at the time. I even did a search on the internet on return 'do ducks eat meat'?

Yes they do! The concern was replaced with 'that's convenient'; much of that which went into the food processor was then disposed of during a few daytime dog walks, into the water to feed the ducks in several locations.

The wasteland rising water area, the river in town, but most was in the public parks of which there are two with ducks. I didn't throw in large amounts at a time in any one location, if they aren't hungry they don't eat it. Any uneaten would be had by vermin but too much in one area clearly would be reckless.

The river here is fenced and separated by a bank, you need to throw hard if inside the park; at the far end where the passage of the monks is sealed, the river is wider and further away from the eye. The ducks sit here on the banks and island, it is not unusual behaviour to feed the ducks. Two bridges in this vicinity cross the river and although easier to drop food down into the water, there was a chance that someone crossing the bridge could notice what one is feeding the ducks with so I didn't take that risk.

In the dark, in the dead of night, in that dead end in silence, I found myself trying to imagine what life was like here all those years ago; how they used the river to bring what was needed, but how did they build such a place back then and did they know the caves were there or did they make them?
Why did they use them and how many got lost in them; does the town stand on various dead individuals that never made it out the other side several miles away?

I imagined what it felt like to be trapped underground, especially back then, no battery torches. When we were kids we entered these caves in two locations, as far as I'm aware no one came to any harm; there are several caves and caverns around here, a network of old lays underneath, they must have been brave people as us kids never went that far in, there was always the element of fear that kept our explorations in check.

Sadly these entrances were sealed off so subsequent generations never got the chance to go in; preserved areas for bats now, but you can still scramble down to a couple and you can look inside through the bars of the large grills and you can put things through the grill.
No one is going in there ever, the entrances were sealed with concrete blocks years ago, the grills are there for the bats and vermin.
This is a tricky place to be at night, without a torch you would fall and break your neck; it's not a completely lonely place, people do pass through here on dog walks, but the signs do warn of the danger.
In those caves, meat and the like would rot and no one would ever know; surrounded by all things natural and creatures, exposed yet shielded, time and nature will take its course.

It was a bit tricky scrambling back up, I'm no spring chicken, the dog made a better job of it than I, had I been seen it made no odds, people do go down there to look, its not at all an uncommon occurrence, but over time the knowledge that you can't really see anything deters people from bothering. The fact that I knew you couldn't was the reason I went down there; I disposed of by posting. Anyway, that's the other side of town from the night dead end; it made me wonder what they were doing way over there and the thought of being underground made me shudder.

People say there are ghosts and there are tales of ghostly figures walking the area at night, they even have ghost tours which is a bit daft as I didn't see any; it isn't creepy, it's just old.

The only noise was the water and the animals and the Westminster chime every 15 minutes, followed on the hour with a slight delay from the clock in the centre of town; the two aren't quite synchronised, the delayed one sometimes seems like the echo of the first but it's not.

I've never walked as much in my entire life as I did during lockdown, every single day and several times a day no matter the weather. I felt a lot healthier for it, lost quite a bit of weight and with every disposal the load was lighter, physically and mentally.

There are indeed many benefits to having a dog, including companionship, fun, cuddly, partner in activities where you'd otherwise do them alone, a listening ear to you and for you, eyes to see things you cannot, super senses that signal attention required, exercise requirements that stop you from being lazy, allow you to act silly in public, to go places that would otherwise look suspicious on one's own, and they love you for you and want nothing more than love, attention and care in return; they don't harm you to please themselves, they don't lie, cheat, deceive; with the added bonus that they love eating meat.

But I must add here that there comes great responsibility, due care and attention and vet bills are massive, so be prepared, but they are worth it. I owe my dog everything.

We weren't really allowed to have pets growing up but I've had a love of animals always; animal cruelty makes me really angry, there should be tougher penalties. As a child both sides of grandparents had a dog, one was spoiled, the other chained to a kennel in the garden; one was friendly the other would bite your face off given the opportunity.
Just an observation but, the grandmother who had led the most horrific life was kind to animals, the other (without morals) saw them as serving a purpose and she literally hated cats.

She had married a man (eventually, after some interesting relationships) who was my mother's step father. I feared him for many many reasons; in the large garden there were ducks, geese, pigeons, chickens, rabbits and the dog chained so that you could not walk past to where the creatures were; his purpose was to guard the garden.
The geese were pretty scary at times and were feared nearly as much as that dog.
As tempting as it was to straddle the fence to see the furry bunnies, one knew at a relatively young age that it would be taking one's life into one's own hands.

This land had two houses, the original, where I am about to depart from and the newer, built on the land where the pond used to be. I grew up between the two and the third house just down the hill, where my dad's parents eventually moved to and settled.

The worst of human behaviours in one road, from where a warped form of symbiosis developed; the two organisms benefiting the other were two houses, the third house then acting like a parasitic organism feeding off the two; a twisted state of equilibrium in family matters.

By the time I hit my teens I was barred from the original house, number 1.

This was for 'telling a terrible lie', that is how that 'family matter' was handled, the truth became a lie; I was to never enter the house again, that was it, the rest went under the carpet and life went on.

No one ever spoke about any of it ever again, looking back now, it isn't surprising considering the secrets in immoral behaviour of my grandmother; did she think it was normal? I will never know.

I don't want to say much about him, just that he was a horrible man.

In respect to all the garden creatures, when I was young I was oblivious to what clipping bird wings was, I must have been backward in not questioning why these ones didn't ever fly.

When I was old enough to be 'sensible' I was tasked with cleaning out the animal houses and I thought I was being helpful in helping out with the animals, I stupidly offered to help take them to market with him; like I've said, no good deed goes unpunished, that's as much as I will say, I'm not going back down that road in my head.

On a note, when I found out or actually realised that these animals were not being traded as pets, I had forty fits which got me more than a hiding for the amount of abusive swear words that was projected over the fence; more to that than met the eye clearly.

My grandmother wasn't a violent person neither was she weak, there was an element of madness and insecurity, I don't know her full story only fragments of her past. My mother wasn't great toward her when she began to die and I'm not sure of the real reasons.

My grandmother's mother (of whom I never knew of course) was a strict religious woman, my mum did speak about the fear of nanny; you couldn't speak at the table, nor look up apparently. She kept a cane on the table and would use it if you made a noise even whilst eating; god fearing, overbearing strict frightening individual by all accounts.

Anyway, my grandmother had a brother and a sister, the sister was a lot younger; the brother went away to war and went to a different country for a long time after; on his return he met the sister, shockingly and horrifyingly, they entered into a relationship and moved in together, moved away and stayed together until death, no children thankfully.

My grandmother kept in contact with them, even staying with them, down by the coast.

My grandmother did marry my grandfather, my mum's dad, but he went away to war and never came back, he was killed in action. This country didn't do anything to help war widows back then; my grandmother and my mum, who was young, lived in poverty because he died in war.

There were stories that my grandmother did things 'in kind' for food stuffs, items of garments and cigarettes.

Apparently the particular place she frequented remained her favorite place until death, and of which she now 'unofficially' lays. The same place I used for the disposal of his heart of stone; maybe she will ensure he suffers, maybe she will ensure the family matter is never uncovered, ensuring the dirty laundry isn't ever aired in public.

Anyway, in this particular place of which she frequented, she met a man (obviously) and they struck up a friendship, my mother remembered playing ball with him; but he went back to his home country (war had ended) and my grandmother took my mum to her brother and sister's (aunt and uncle, literally!) down by the sea.
This secret didn't come out for many many years, but she gave birth down there and the baby went to the other side of the world; this came back to get her just before she died; maybe this is one of the reasons why my mum ignored her suffering and let her die alone. The 'dying alone' became a theme and no doubt I will go the same way.

My grandmother and mum had nowhere to live so my grandmother took a job as a housekeeper in another town, it was live in and she took my mum who was not yet at school; my grandmother eventually left that job taking away more than wages, another baby! Having nowhere to go, she went back home to her god fearing mother and put the baby up for adoption; she had managed 3 babies by 3 different fathers by then (that we were aware of) however, she pulled out of the adoption when she was housed locally.
Apparently the two children were led a dog's life as she was mentally unstable.
One day she 'lost the plot' so to speak and she was put in a mental institution with a nervous breakdown. The children were taken into a children's home and separated whilst there; stories from that in itself wouldn't surprise you I'm sure but it had the biggest effect on the younger of the two, she grew up not coping well, had a child she was terribly mean to, of which I witnessed on growing up; but like I've said, this was all normal.
The chain of behaviour went on and on, just as well it is almost at an end.

Anyway, eventually my grandmother got well and the children went home; but it continues, my grandmother took a job of looking after the house and boys of a man whose wife had died; you've guessed it, she fell pregnant again, but this time she married him, gave up her house and the families became blended with much older boys. My grandmother was caught having relations with the oldest of these boys, but this was kept in the family, literally.

All this information growing up simply instills in one that people are never who they present themselves as. To the outside world, there was never anything to see here.

When that old man died, he died alone in the back bedroom, here, in this house, 1 narcissist road; he used to turn the light switch on and off with his walking stick, sometimes in the dead of night I hear that light switch even when the room is empty.

When he died all the animals were taken to market, the garden uprooted, a massive fire raged of all the hutches, sheds, enclosures. For weeks the pigeons and doves flew back, like a daily haunting, but bit by bit it stopped as they realised there was nothing to come back to. The dog died not long after but I have my doubts surrounding that, no one could handle it as it was his and the poor thing was never a pet.

A few years later, two of those boys (grown men by then) died within 8 months of each other, both dropped dead of a heart attack, ending those ties to this house; the other had long ago gone abroad vowing never to return (he didn't) as he hated my grandmother; at this point we all merged on the one house, allowing the relocation of the grandparents nextdoor; the walls were closing in and the family began eating itself up, and age aided the speed of death.

They all died alone aside from my dad but he was in the hospital and like I've said, he made a terrible fuss about it, the opposite to silence.

So, like I've said, we didn't do pets as kids and cats were hated by my grandmother who instilled a fear of cats in my mum, who carried this on into adulthood; really quite stupid.

I still hold my mum responsible for the death of tommy; I've no idea if he ever had a name or if he ever had a home, but back then there weren't such things as the cat's protection or the like, he was probably a street cat. He wasn't allowed in the house but was allowed to be fed outside, he had one eye, was friendly and quite large, but he may not have been, I was a kid.

He was around for some years and had a bed of old jumpers and cardys stuffed into cardboard boxes. It sat in the outside porch area and was frequently kicked off; the parents didn't have the same compassion for animals, it's a wonder they tolerated the feeding of him. That particular winter was harsh, it was freezing. The milkman left the milk, it would freeze sending the milk out the top of the bottle, pushing the tops off, forming stalks of frozen milk with glistening hats. The cat would lick this, mum would go mad; but it grew colder and colder. I begged her to let the cat in the back room, which was more like an indoor shed as it contained the gas and electric meters, the back door, a concrete floor and brick walls.

It was treated like an indoor shed for bikes, shoes, garden tools; it was large and I'm still none the wiser as to if it was intentional or a non complete build.

Anyway, they refused point blank to let the cat in. Tommy froze to death on the doorstep, he froze because of her; I was so upset. She opened the door to get the milk, she was shouting and going ahead, the milkman had set the milk bottles down behind the cat and she couldn't get the milk because of the effing dead cat.

Dad threw Tommy into the hedgerow of the alleyway; I cried a lot and was very angry. Getting ready for school I was told off for crying; I hit my mum 18 times with my hairbrush, how do I know it was 18?

Because she counted and slapped my legs the same amount of times.

After school I went and got Tommy out of the hedge, I put him in a bag with a blanket; his box and stuff had already gone. I tried to dig a hole in the garden to bury him, in my naivety, I didn't know about frozen ground when it's freezing. It was solid, it was never going to happen no matter how long I tried.

My mum took the bag and put it in the dustbin; I was disturbed by that so I took the bag back out, walked to the cemetery but the gates were shut, it was almost dark so I went back home with the cat in the bag and put him in the shed. In the morning, on the way to school, I got the bag and went to the cemetery, it's five minutes from the house, I knew where I was going as us kids had put things down there 100 times.

Looking back, that was not a nice thing to do and isn't funny, I don't know why we thought putting rubbish and stuff down the side of the old grave tomb was funny, but that's by the by. Tommy was buried with a long dead person whose grave is just about recognisable today. There are now many of these with broken and shifted tops where rabbits pop out from time to time and to where it is extremely easy to pop things down, unnoticed.

I spent my whole life trying to fathom people, why they do the things they do; since I did what I did, I realise that there's no simple answer.

It's because, because, because; many things affect many things, the domino effect with infinite runways going off in infinite directions, never ending as those dominoes fall with every move we make and with everything we say.

One cannot predict how it falls nor in which direction; even a brief eye meet between two people can alter a thought and the domino falls a nanometer to the left and changes something of what was about to happen; people are as unpredictable as they are predictable.

Competition versus cooperation, generational trauma handed down and around; concentric circles influencing conversations, relationships, experiences.

But those influences cannot cause all outcomes, the actions come from within, prompted by what and why depends on the moment in time.

Moments in time..I remember many from my long life, not all bad. I like most people remember the best times and the worst times; it's obvious why we remember the worst, they cause trauma which tends to lurk around and we struggle to suppress it, that is understandable.

But I wonder sometimes, why I remember particular moments that I perceive as good times, why those? What made them so different? 9 out of 10 times of those moments would have been tainted directly before or directly after, that's how things were; so why do I get a partial warm glow thinking of them?

Has my mind photo-snapped moments in time and relocated them, purposefully taken them out of context to fill up the memory file (good memories) with pretty pictures, it's objective being to have some kind of carbon offset.

Creating a perfect photo album of good things to match that of the bad, maybe!

I do find it strange and consider my mind is controlled and arranged by something other than me. If I'm the conscious, who is the subconscious? Odd thought no doubt.

I remember childhood christmas days, the smell of pine, lime cordial, satsumas; I know these memories are jumbled. The tradition of an absolutely massive tree was from my dad's side, they used to cut them down and bring them in; not in this country, these came off the market and were delivered.

Christmas was one day, boxing day was the grandparents.

When we were young we were sent to bed early christmas eve, yes that's normal, but I bet your mother didn't wallpaper the lounge overnight. We would come down in the morning to a freshly wallpapered lounge, a massive decorated tree and of course presents.

The new wallpaper would have all the christmas cards pinned to it on a large expanse by the door; as I got older I observed the pin holes that sat there for the entire year until the next christmas eve; by the time we were older and aged relatives had died off, that strange tradition ceased and of course we left that house, and 1a became no more.

I will never know why my mum exhausted herself the night before the big day. Was she aiming to photosnap a perfect pretty picture for her good memory file, as she knew full well the big day always went to rack and ruin.

My memory of lime cordial is due to my dad mixing it with lager, he would consume enough to enable him to have his face fall into his dinner.

Mum spent most of the day either cooking or asleep or breaking up arguments. Christmas day looked pretty, that's about it really and I don't know why the smell of satsumas brings any of that back.

One christmas I was given the biggest dolls house but the stupid sibling slid down the roof and bust it, what he received after tainted that day, but that's just one of many; but there must have been happy moments or I wouldn't remember them in the good file or maybe life was so up and down daily that one's mind grabbed at the good and kept it even if it were a fleeting moment.

Like I've said, not everything in my life has been bad, I've seen and done a lot, much of my adventures have happy snapshots, I can pull many out the hat right now and am grateful for those times; whilst I've not been able to travel the world (not many have) I have seen plenty and I hope my new life allows for more.

We get one life, we can't come back and try it again, I've wasted much of mine and realised too late, but it's not too late for you. My plan is, like they say, hope for the best, prepare for the worst.

My mum did neither, she sat on some strange autopilot, brushed everything under the carpet and her life slipped away. I don't hate her for allowing bad things to happen then ignoring the effects; how can I? I went on and did the very same; bad mothers but mothers nonetheless.

People overlook mothers, mothers are people too, individuals with stories, not just mums and wives and daughters and granddaughters; why were we expected to give up everything for everyone else anyway? Why were we expected to be the carers, the domestic, the shopper, the forever on duty person and hold down a job as well; why were we expected to only think and feel for others and forget ourselves? Where did it get us anyway; after wasting our lives we end up too old to do the things we could have.

Just look at how many old mums get chucked into the old folks homes now. This era dictates that once you've served your purpose you become a liability and a burden of which only a care home can see to.

So tell me, what's the point in giving your all then ending your days incarcerated?

No thank you, prison or care home, same institutional regime. I've worked in hundreds whilst working agencies, some of the truths would make you sick.

I didn't put any relative into a care home despite the past, like I've said, I'm not dark triad; if I wanted revenge that bad, I could subtly do it myself without the help of an institution.

So, the good moments that I'm grateful for include; lemon meringue pie, dropped scones and maple syrup, cheese straws, bread and butter pudding, cold custard and chocolate buttons, packets of plain dry biscuits and cold cooked potatoes.

The lemon meringue pie and dropped scones belong to my dad's mum, the bread and butter pudding and cheese straws belong to my mum's mum; the dry biscuits and cold cooked potatoes are due to us being latchkey kids, who ever got home first after school got the only available food stuffs until later that evening, if at all, shift depending.

You wouldn't believe the fights and arguments we had over cold potatoes left in a saucepan on the stove; why is that in the good memory? being triumphant and eating it with glee and free of parents time, therefore no wits about you required.

Playing music, switching the tv over, running around in an unruly manner; as long as we didn't create a huge noise level, no attention was drawn to next door and no nosey grandparent would bust in.

I guess they are good moments as they were moments of freedom; the growing up moments of spreading wings and seeing things and going away on school trips; we all went on every single one and kitted out with new clothes and accessories, contributed to by all three houses, we even went on the extra highly expensive trips including a cruise around the mediterranean.

like I've said, we presented well.

My good moments also include, central park, the hudson, macey's at christmas, the plaza, china town, empire state, rockefeller, times square; french chateaus, old towns on hills, houses built into rocks, sleeping in a cave (troglodytes), amphitheatres, the acropolis, old dubrovnik, the vatican, basilica, catacombs, kasbahs, coliseum, watching the sun go down on the seas, staying up and watching the sun come up, warms seas, warm sand, travelling through countries and exploring cultures, pisa, chianti, St Tropez, Nice, eating fish BBQ'd on the beach, running in the opposite direction of the wild boar, monaco, montecarlo, barcelona, driving through fields of lavender and tasting it in the wine, roller coasters, sand dunes, tea rooms, laughing until I cried, crying until I laughed.

The kids faces when young on christmas morning, riding their bikes without stabilisers, and there I have to stop; I am no longer a mother. All good moments will have to go away along with all the bad.

Everything that has gone before is now irrelevant. No one exists anymore to relate to any of it, all moments are now surplus to requirements; I can't take them with me, hence wiping the slate clean. When I leave I cannot take any of it with me, all of that belongs to somebody else, it is no longer mine.

I stopped listening to music and I stopped watching tv, I did this to halt the triggers, to help in my transition. Transformation is not easy, to say it has all been easy would be a lie and that's not what all this confession is about; the truth matters in order to allow me to move on and away to end my days without fear or drama. To let go of my entire past means I would no longer be living the life whereby that song would be most fitting 'all kinds of everything remind me of you'...'summertime, wintertime, spring and autumn too...monday, tuesday, everyday, I think of you'. That's what remaining here all these years was like, patterns repeating themselves from previous generations; imbalance in everything, within these walls, within narcissist road.

Changing is uncomfortable, it has been a challenge, the limitation it turns out, was my human and very strange mind all along. When one is trapped in warped m-fields of the dark triads and one's tolerance fills to the brim, and there's no healthy outlet for pent up emotions, there creates some drastic damaging effects; one ends up allowing things to happen that should not be tolerated, until one day, one moment, one can take no more, and that one moment, one action, changes the way the domino falls; with that one smash in the face of brute, that domino runway took off in the direction of the unimagined.

Moments in time, that of which I have many, will remain behind when I go. All the things I've seen and done I will forget, I will never speak of nor think of any once this has been written; but heed what I say here about institutional care homes and about chucking your family member in one. My 'family' was deranged, damaging and dysfunctional but none entered the walls of a care home, not one; I don't have the guilt from that.

I intend to fully forget what I've seen whilst working in them; they aren't all horrific but they are all pretty much institutional, it's a fact.
Why is this country so reliant on these facilities?
Why is it now the norm to offload the elderly into them?
When did it become acceptable to displace these people, I don't understand.
We have devalued the very people that made the country in which you live today, raised you, taught you, sat up all night with you, or maybe not. Nevertheless they got you a fair way into life, then you chuck them in the bin.

The selfish generations of the nuclear family, materialistic and competitive; life is so busy that you can't see to your own mum's basic needs, someone else has that job.
You spend your lives with your faces stuck in your phone screens, order food in or go out to eat, you consider yourselves trendy folk as you attend a gym or go running; all whilst your elderly parent is sitting in some overused, and possibly urine stained chair in the corner of a lounge in some institution that dictates when they are hungry and when they are tired, I just don't understand.

Look what happened to these people in lockdown, literally locked away weren't they, forced vaccines, restricted lives in an already restricted environment; outstandingly outrageous. I cannot even begin to think of what their lives were like, and for some, sadly ended their days incarcerated.

Not all countries put their elderly in care homes, I've seen it with my own two eyes, large families looking after them, all sitting around large tables, the elderly being valued. But that's not our country's culture is it, and I haven't seen it much here either.

Seeing things that I didn't like, that I knew were wrong, disturbed me; I didn't know any of those people, their pasts, nothing, but it was my job to deliver care professionally with dignity and respect, of which I did. I wouldn't have dreamt of leaving them to die alone or to wait, it wasn't personal, it was professional, which means being objective, not subjective, personal shouldn't come into it; for me that was how I worked.

But some staff didn't, some would express their thoughts and opinions and would treat the 'service user' accordingly; liked them, fine, didn't like them, not nice. It used to make me angry but after working in many many different 'homes', I realised I was banging my head against a brick wall when I pointed something out. I was agency, sent to do a job, not to have an opinion let alone express it; not to stick my nose in and rock the boat "Who did I think I was"?

Don't get me wrong, not all homes are badly run with a bad culture, but most are run on a shoestring and rarely enough staff. One home I walked into, I turned around and walked out, I made a phone call and was told I wouldn't be sent back there, fine, but they sent someone else instead. So it had fallen on deaf ears and money came before welfare.

On stepping into the lounge area of this home, my shoes stuck to the carpet, this wasn't a confined area, it was the entire carpet; it smelled and when I looked around I saw an elderly lady sitting in a filthy chair with her head tilted backwards and her mouth open (this does happen with some ailments) But, there were flies all around her and they were going in and out of her open mouth, she couldn't move to stop this. If you are not shocked and repulsed by this then I'm afraid you are of dark triad.

I frantically waved my hands about her head to deter the flies, it didn't work; I went to a permanent member of staff and pointed this out, I was told not to worry, it happened all the time and she (the elderly lady) doesn't even notice. What a shocker no? I walked out, I never went back.

Another time I was sent to a place and sent to the top floor, dementia floor, to discover I was working on my own. There were people walking about, it was a night shift and I had no idea what even their names were or what room belonged to whom. I went down a floor to find the person on duty was also agency; down to the bottom, I found an agency staff that worked there frequently. Her answer was, the files are locked away from agency staff, but not to worry as the residents would probably not go to bed all night and if they do they will know their rooms. Now this sounds unbelievable doesn't it, but let me tell you this was quite common.

Many a shift in many establishments were worked solely by agency, some knew what they were doing, some didn't. It was the luck of the draw if you worked with staff that knew, if you were lucky (and the residents) you were informed and could do your job properly. The irony here is that us agency at the time were on far more money than the absent permanent, yet half the time we were chucked in at the deep end and tried to wing it.

I've worked in homes where I was the only native speaking staff as the 'home' had recruited overseas; whilst this made little difference to the care given as I can't say I saw much wrongdoing there, but I had no idea what they were saying all shift as I didn't speak their language. And if i didn't know what they were saying, I'm as sure as sugar the residents didn't either. Another place I was sent to, I worked there for a while, it was a well known company but run on low amounts of staff of which some weren't the most pleasant of people. There was a staff member that wasn't particularly caring, she voiced her opinions in saying things like "his family don't visit as he's a nasty piece of work" "no one bothers with her as she isn't a nice person" "it's obvious why he doesn't get visitors" "I'm not doing him, he's awkward on purpose, he doesn't like me" "have I got her again? For god's sake"

This was all ignored, it was the norm. I could never make out why that staff member would volunteer to stay with residents (people) for their passing; if she was on duty that's what she did, sat with them whilst they passed away. She was known to come in early and stay late for these happenings. I used to have fleeting thoughts about her motives, what did she say to them? I hope the last thing they heard was not something horrible from her vile mouth.

Or was it because it meant she just had to sit there; but it used to bother me, however one couldn't just accuse and since no one else voiced a concern I considered I may have had paranoia but it made no good sense to me, and as they say, it takes one to recognise one.

That same home would have many residents in bed before 6pm if particular staff were on the night shift or indeed if there was a staff shortage on the night shift, which was more often than not. One staff per wing to put to bed quite a number of residents (people).

What occurred was 'the norm', pad changes without washing, night clothes hurriedly put on without washing nor the creams applied that were meant to be, but the care plan was ticked that they had been; and without concern for stiff joints. Once someone's leg was cut as one person did what should have been two staff via hoist, there was no hoist and only one person so they lifted and it went wrong, but no one batted an eyelid, it wasn't unusual.

An institutional regime of being woken, breakfast in bed before attending to the toilet, then a round of whipping off night clothes, sheep dip, clothes on, into wheelchairs, into the day room. Cup of tea, bed changes, toileting time (that's what it's termed) back to day room, lunch time, toileting time, lounge time; activities or not, maybe just tv. Activities of throwing and catching balls, giant sticky darts or some other ludicrous childlike game for a person with a lifetime of experience; supper time, toileting time, bed time. And people paid for this service.

Another home I went to, not many times as I refused; I was seeing to a man who had come out of hospital, he wasn't talking and was curled up on the bed, very frail. The 'senior' came in, I had taken him a cup of tea, she spoke to him, he didn't answer. She told me he hadn't spoken since coming back from hospital, I said perhaps it hurts him to speak? She said no, he is sulking. She spoke to him again, he didn't answer, so she took the tea away and said "you can have a drink when you can bloody well answer me", she left (with the cup of tea).
I reported this to the manager, who told me the senior was a valued staff member and knew what she was doing. Who was I to argue being agency, what did I know? Well, I know what cruelty is and that was cruelty in order to have control.

The frail, the sick, the weary, the alert, the downtrodden, the stubborn, the brow beaten with an entire lifetime of living and giving, end their days at the mercy of someone else's mood, belief, preconceptions and institutional culture.

Asking to go to the toilet, asking for a drink, having to wait until someone is free to help or willing to help; being left in wet and soiled pads, being told to use the pad "that's what it's for"; basically you're in bed, you're wearing a pad so go ahead and wet yourself as "there's not enough staff", "it will waste the pad", "your care doesn't pay for night service".

Left in wheelchairs until blood supply is cut off in the legs, force fed blended crap and if the staff is in a hurry, go ahead and choke as more and more is shoved in without a chance to swallow.

Inappropriate language, manual handling techniques that went out with the arc, staff talking over the heads of people whilst whipping off their clothes; talking on their mobile phones, scrolling on social media, talking in different languages, rough handling, shut in rooms on purpose, alarms and call buttons moved out of reach, fake entries on food and fluid charts, bullshit written in the daily care plan; I've seen it all and it bothered me enough to remove myself from the system.

Controlling people, uncaring people, and those that informed me of what CARE stood for..

Cover Arse Remain Employed. The job you do when there's nothing else about. It's not skilled and you don't even need to actually care, just show up. Such was the shortage of staff, created by the culture of chucking the elderly away into profit making establishments.

But of course not all staff were uncaring and not all establishments are totally bad; but now the pandemic has given rise to a worsening situation as has Brexit. I cannot imagine what it must be like now with further staff shortages and distancing restrictions, what a way to end your life.

If the families kept their elderly and collectively cared for them, the business of care wouldn't exist would it; it wasn't as rife when I was growing up, so what happened? And why did companies need to do recruitment drives overseas? Was it due to cheaper labour? Did they tie them into not so great contracts? Was it due to the country's indigenous population being unwilling to work those god awful hours? I don't know, but I do know that this country does not have a good work life balance, the weather on the whole is not great, there's no outdoor living in the sun that's for sure, I am glad that I am leaving. It rains too much, it's oppressive, one doesn't live, one merely exists; not really any stunning views, it's not sun drenched with clean sands and seas, the culture is driven by 'live to work' instead of 'work to live'.

I question the migrant workers on what possesses them to partake in this dull land of drudgery; many say it's beneficial in sending money home where their currency is worth less. So I guess if your sole purpose is to come and earn to build better back home then I can see the reasoning, for them there is probably an end in sight; otherwise if you are a citizen and no plan to migrate and you aren't wealthy, then what is there to look forward to?
Retirement to a care institution? But before even getting there you may be lucky enough to make it to retirement, since they keep moving the retirement age, it will likely mean work until you drop dead, and they hope so, they won't have to pay your pension.

But if you survive it is likely you will pay the price by being incarcerated and if you are extremely unlucky a pandemic may take you off whilst you're there.

Maybe in a few years time they will have achieved their aim by decreasing the population; shrink wrapped the NHS and sold it off; leaving this island to be a data colony where the vaccinated, chipped and programmed (Human Augmentation look it up on the government website) worker bees buzz about and elderly no longer exists; just saying.

YOU AREN'T GOING BACK TO NORMAL:

People still believe their pre-pandemic lives will return, they think that this time next year everything will be back to 'normal'.
Normal that we knew is not ever going to return, certainly not for me by a long shot, but not for you either.
It isn't just my life that has changed, although not your typical circumstance, you've not killed anyone have you. Well, that would depend on who is reading this of course, as those that did what they did with their powers surrounding this 'pandemic' did kill people and it was intentional, subtly done in the disguise of a virus; an intentional culling that they will never be held accountable for.
Whilst most of the population hung on every word of the mainstream media, believing the men in suits on their tv; others dug out documents and research papers, policies, correspondence including emails. They tried to tell everyone what was really happening but they were vilified and publicly shot down. Let me reiterate here, your life will not ever go back to your normal.
You need to get your head around what is coming; prepare yourselves.
I don't know if these things will happen before or after I send this out there, but the markets are going to be crashed; they are going to take down certain crypto currencies; the banking system will change, countries will have their own crypto currencies and you will end up banking with the state.

They will know every penny you have, where it came from, what you spend it on, if you are making healthy choices; they will deny your unhealthy habits, they will cancel things that you cannot afford, they will deny you services for bad choices and reward you for being good; cash is going, they can't control cash.

Your identity will be digital, it will be combined with your financial status and your health status; your DNA will predict your worth and your likely outcome.

The aim is global ID, global governance, no money laundering or hoarding, no dark web, no cash in hand, no under market, no fraud. Deterrence of terrorism, threats, danger.

Apparently.. purified air, clean waters, no hunger, no poverty; your physical footprint will be taken and replaced by a virtual one.. enter the fourth industrial revolution.

But to achieve all that, their own corruption has to get past other's corruption, so the future is going to be one big upheaval; there will be supply problems, power struggles, food shortages, further restrictions, mandatory vaccinations, boosters, issues with meat, financial & crypto struggles.

A prediction from the 'First global Revolution' 1991: The monied and the powers to be will fight it out and turmoil will spread globally.

In brief, what I am referring to, in case you have no idea of any of the talk, the argument, the protests and some of the things that people are afraid of: The Great Rest, maybe you have heard of this, maybe not.

A very brief description: The WEF: The World Economic Forum, which has it's own website, in case you aren't aware.

It communicates with the world, publishes, makes decisions, influences. An international organisation headquartered in Geneva, Switzerland; meetings held at Davos to discuss the world.

Davos meetings attended by the elite, politicians, academics, media owners, intellectuals, influential organisations, scientists, religious leaders, royalty and the like; it is a powerful transnational corporation of elites and zillionaires.

There are other groups that people mention along with the WEF but I will just keep this simple and brief. What scares some people are the agendas that have been in the making for years and that are now coming to fruition; Agenda 2030, ID2020 and so on; and the things that the WEF have published and indeed have said recently.

Some believe that the world's elite have a sinister plan to control the entire world; It is known as the New World Order.
New World, New Normal, New Reality. The Globalists.
People are scared of the loss of control over their lives, the control going to these elite decision makers.

The WEF haven't hidden their plans, they are all there, out in the open to read, and even Klaus Schwab (the founder) wrote and published a book in the early months of the 'pandemic'.. 'Covid-19 The Great Reset'.

The WEF have had plans and agendas for years; all now being implemented under the guise of the virus (covid)

But during the pandemic these elites made trillions of pounds / dollars and people believe that the involved corporations are now more powerful than countries and individual nations; that globalisation will maximise their power, especially big tech and that we will all have to be compliant.

The WEF wish to build entirely new foundations for economic and social systems;
AI, quantum computing; in using covid to bring in all planned changes including to harness the innovations of the fourth industrial revolution.

They ask us to adjust our mindset and accept the coming changes. It states on its website: The reset initiative: to use this unique moment (covid) in history, provided by the disruptions (covid) to our economics, politics and everyday lives to catalyse a new approach to how our societies run. (preplanned)
They quote: The pandemic represents a rare but narrow window of opportunity to reflect, re-imagine and reset our world.
Some say that the WEF weaponised covid to have us all into submission; WEF the front for all involved. Some say it isn't real, some say it was released intentionally via a GOF (gain of function) experiment in a lab, a pre planned culling; in order to bring in all the planned changes, to which otherwise the population would not have accepted.

But the fact is we will never know. Whatever the truth, we can't do much about it, change is happening, there's no going back.

In 2014 the WEF called for a reshaping of the world and have recently stated…
We cannot simply go back to normal. What was once considered essential is now superfluous. Nothing will ever return to the broken sense of normalcy that prevailed prior to the crises. (covid)
WEF's fourth industrial revolution, they say, supports the public good.

Building green cities, reducing physical footprints to virtual, a technological takeover. Digital ID encompassing all aspects of our information, we will just be a bunch of data and lands will become data colonies.

Some people believe that this global agenda will take over national soverentities, control movements of populations and impose world wide programmes.

People have expressed fears in saying that the great reset is linked to the climate crisis and some say there is no climate crisis; they express their fear in saying that the reset is in motion timed with the release of the papers 'climate crisis moment 2020' in saying that the unelected unaccountable elites (who jet around the world and into space) are attempting global control, in their belief that humans have overrun the planet and requires depopulation.

It is believed that in order to bring in the changes, and to stave off civil unrest, they paused us by bringing in restrictions and lockdowns; and that they have manufactured a virus and injections to solve the overpopulation problem.

It is also believed that by 2025 many of us will not be living. I cannot vouch for any of that and neither can I say that there is or is not a climate crisis or over population problem.

Back in 2011: James Delingpole wrote about The Global Warming Conspiracy (The Goal Is Power). He said (amongst others; Climategate Scandal) global warming is a fraud, one that costs billions of dollars and is a clear and present danger to our liberty. Points out: manipulated data, suppression of evidence that contradicts the hypothesis of global warming; suppression of opposition by squeezing dissenting scientists out of peer review (hasn't that currently happened with covid?)

He said: global warming is not about science but about politics, the expanding power of elites using the coercive instruments of government to control the lives of people everywhere; increasing their power to rule over the rest of us.

Having considered that, what are peoples thoughts on weather manipulation?
No one really talks about that do they. But it has been happening for years and is widely documented.
Now there are papers and opinions on weather warfare; Not everyone is even aware that the weather can be manipulated, if you aren't, look it up yourself. The next time it rains for days on end, consider the question, has this occurred naturally?

These current issues with floods and fires all over the place, one has to wonder if they are all natural happenings, as the timing with the so-called climate crisis moment 2020 is a tad suspicious is it not?
In my own thoughts, I believe that too much is happening all at the same time: pandemic, climate, floods, fires, economies, changing banking systems, injections, health passports, restrictions and never ending propaganda.
Thankfully I don't have a TV, I don't listen day in day out. I'm not brainwashed, not yet.
But all the barrage comes from the elite, telling us what is best for us.

Consider also, how do these elite wealthy people live so long?
Standards of living yes of course, but some of these people get to very old ages, maintaining fitness, don't they.

In my researching, after I did what I did, I came across the knowledge of a drug.

The drug is not available to the general population, well of course it isn't, we are overpopulated!

The drug is anti aging, SRT 1720 Hydrochloride: costs hundreds of dollars and is apparently only available for research purposes. But one has to wonder.

So there we are, if you can afford it and know a person who knows a person, maybe you too can have a long long life. Just saying.

I did not plan the timing of my actions, but they couldn't have been timed better if I'd have tried; gone before I'm chipped here, they can do that from my new life. I don't want their chip nor their vaccine but I doubt I will have an option, but initially there will be so much going on that I will pale into insignificance.

Maybe the new way of life, that of which will be more controlled will give me something to think about and aid me to forget the past; wouldn't it be great if their plans for humans included having your mind wiped, a re-set of the brain.

It isn't impossible, look at what they aim to do with Human Augmentation.

The document sits on the government's website, hiding in plain sight.

They've been testing these chips with little monkeys and they've been messing about with DNA to literally change it; who knows, maybe they can change who you are by altering the DNA, they can already stitch together different strands of dna and have already created different organisms; but changing your dna is a bit in the future so don't be too concerned just yet, just fear the brain chip for now as that will ensure your compliance.

INTERNET OF BODIES:
INTERNET OF THINGS:

When 5g is in full swing all autonomy over oneself will be gone. 5g is required for Internet of Bodies (IOB) Internet Of Things (IOT) enabling more and more devices to connect to each other at greater speed; 5g can support one million devices per square foot, get your head around that one.

Wifi 6 will improve connectivity and more devices to transmit data. Thousands of satellites orbiting the earth (the earth that they say is in climate crisis) will enable the Internet Of Things technology, for example smart home systems, to connect to the IOB devices, which in turn increases digital tracking.

Currently being developed, augmented reality contact lenses (yikes) and direct brain interfaces, which will alter your social life as well as record your interactions; neuro devices, brain interfaces, brain reading, will mean brain writing; which could obviously affect one's thoughts, meaning the technology can be used for both good and bad purposes to do harm, including maybe in warfare.

IOB used in the military will enhance the individual's capabilities, adjusting whatever the body requires and one could say enabling a human drone. Flying planes via thought control will be used by brain interfacing with the plane; the US Department of Defence already has an infrared laser that can detect cardiac signature from 200 meters.

By 2025 (there's that significant year) there will be over 40 billion active IOT devices connecting to and interacting with the environment, transport, geolocations, diet, exercise, biosensors, social activity and so on; basically all aspects of all our lives.

IOB will mean less medical care is required and will be less expensive on already overburdened healthcare systems, but it will also mean that one can be snuffed out just as easily; think about that.
The entire internet of all things will connect to all those still on grid and will be able to control body and mind. All of that is fact not fiction, fact being stranger than fiction.

Whether one has gone off grid by 2025 will mean nothing as I am pretty sure one could still be located and be visited by a drone.

So much has been developed in a short space of time (that we are aware of) and if it is correct information and the vaccines do contain graphene, then one wonders what will that actually mean?
Graphene has been noted for it's role in the IOT and IOB due to it's unusual properties. Graphene based implantable sensors are currently used in neuroscience but studies have shown toxicity for chronic exposure; currently studies on biocompatibility are still controversial (toxicity to cells associated with direct interaction with cell membrane).
It is also known that there are risks to the environment. Graphene and it's derivatives including graphene oxide (GO) and reduced GO have extraordinary properties: ultra thin, ultrahigh carrier mobility, excellent electrical conductivity, superior thermal conductivity, surface area, high optical transmittance, high young's modulus, outstanding mechanical flexibility.

Much research is available in respect to it's uses in drug delivery, health monitoring systems and interface to the human body: sensors, wearable, implantable for detecting and measuring various signals / analyles.
There are plenty of papers for you to read yourself and it is documented that graphene will be used for the IOB.

However, recent studies that have looked at the toxicity have included the immune system and there is evidence that it can cross physiological barriers and reach secondary organs away from the initial entry and currently there is no data on the long term accumulation effects.
I am very wary of the technological takeover.

Once upon a time it was religion that controlled most of the populations, but over time, on the whole, religion has lost following in the not so wealthy, whereas on the whole the wealthy and self-enhanced attend church to give the illusion that they are good people, but these wealthy mainly have double standards and I have to say can be hypocrites. (although traditional ways of living without religion did survive).

As science and tech has taken over, people's beliefs have evolved. I would like to say something about religion and it is in respect to the current situation with the pandemic.

It may offend some but that is not my intention, I don't wish to take away people's beliefs and I am not poking fun; believe me when I say that I prayed many a time when I was young, I prayed to God and I prayed to Jesus to make it stop but neither heard me.

I was young when I concluded that they didn't exist but still respected that others around me believed they did.

Such is the drop in religion that they, whoever they are, decided that the BC Before Christ and AD Anno Domini (latin: In the year of our lord) system is no longer useful and have replaced this with BCE before current era and CE current era, to divide world history.

I am not saying that particular people in history did not exist, I am pretty sure they did but I don't believe in the whole Abraham happening, which is meant to explain how religion began with one person and sons became divided; aside from that, it appears that religions are causing wars aren't they, so one wonders, are the powers to be doing away with religion?

My point is, if you can get most of the world's population believing in a god, that of which they cannot see, then it would be relatively easy to do the same with fear of a deadly virus.

It is said that the neolithic revolution eleven thousand years ago brought the invention of agriculture which transformed societies from 'hunter gatherer' to a more sedentary lifestyle, creating societies of thousands all in one place. To keep control of large societies is far harder than that of the original smaller groups of a hundred or so; it was here that it is believed big gods who punished bad people came about, prosocial behaviour.

The way to ensure people cooperate is to tell them they are being watched and judged, in order to maintain control.

Hunter gatherer societies don't have organised religion; the last being the Hadza people of Tanzania, a population with no religion aside from acknowledging what they can see, sun, moon, stars, ancestors. They don't keep track of time and age, there is no hierarchy, they have gender equality; they do smoke cannabis and follow a traditional way of life, after all this time and in being encroached upon by pastoralists, land stolen and restrictions placed upon them. Their small groups of living together and the mechanisms used to keep order in their communities, talking and negotiation, is easier.

It is thought also that reasoning people (which they use within their groups) are less likely to believe in a higher intelligence / being.

The cultural evolution of farming / agriculture saw bigger societies develop where people were strangers; anonymous societies required control, the watchful gods, thus organised religion grew with the rise of large societies.

Human existence depends on cooperation, but with who and for whom?
It is known that synchronised activity in groups leads to releases of endorphins; these opioid hormones ease tension and amplify prosocial behaviour, maybe attending religious services with others achieves this and gives people the belief that one god has a big plan and it aids people with some sense of order and control that they feel they need; and that they are accepted by others in that group, a sense of belonging, that they are not alone, it gives them an explanation of life and purpose.

Now, I am not saying the current virus does not exist, I am sure it does actually, but is it as deadly to the entire world as it is made out to be?

No, I don't believe so. **But that literally is my opinion, not a fact. I am quite often wrong**.

What makes people sit up and listen, what makes people easy to control? **Fear**.

That is a fact. Fear or being punished by god, purgatory (I do hope this does exist) controls what one does and unites one with others; as has this pandemic, fear of a virus that will kill you if you don't behave in certain ways and unites the like minded, all of which are being controlled.

So, what if the virus was actually created in a lab by way of gain of function experiments (GOF) which enhance a virus to make it more virulent; to let's say reduce the population and control the rest whilst bringing in changes that would otherwise not be accepted?

Technological takeover.

Technologically advanced society, driven by science (not god) tells us that the world works by the laws of physics not by the hands of a god.

Japan has one of the highest living standards in the world and only a very small percentage is still religious; Japan and Western Europe have universal healthcare and social safety networks, therefore, people rely more on the state than religion.

So have we entered a war between technology and religion? If so, will religion use technologically advanced ways to fight back?

At the end of the day, it is all about control, control of states vs global and beliefs. **So, prepare yourselves, you aren't going back to normal, there are turbulent times ahead, let that sink in.**
I won't be the only one 'starting again', people will begin to flee when they realise what is actually happening.

If you've got something to hide, don't rest on your laurels, they will be coming for you; every bank account will be looked at by the state, govcoins will be used to enable access to your accounts, tax evasion, benefit fraud, whatever, they will find it.

Moving money without being noticed will become a thing of the past. If you've done something that you shouldn't of, now is the time to go, by this time next year it will be too late. If you want to change countries do it now otherwise you will be stuck here, only the wealthy will get off.

Those in the know with all the wealth, already bought up land in particular countries; they've built underground bunkers in places like Newzealand, they didn't do this for the fun of it or through boredom and they aren't holiday homes. So why did they?

That's all I'm saying about all that as I'm sure by now you may think I'm crazy, that's if you can't be bothered to research, it's all out there to find.
Had I not done what I did, I would have been none the wiser on all of the above.

I've told you, I've done my bit, but not as a good deed; the more that move around, the more displacement, the better for me.

I'm looking forward to my new life, whatever it brings; I know I won't be on 'alert' all the time, I won't constantly be in 'fight or flight' mode; I don't have to pretend or lie about falling over to explain purple marks on my face. Even though I knew it was unacceptable, it was my 'normal', it was all I had ever known from very young, it was normal.

For me there is no more walking on eggshells with a front saying I'm just like you with my inner knowing different; I am very pleased that I am never going back to normal.
No more face on, face off, no more different versions of myself, although I'm yet to discover who I really am.
The me has been manufactured, molded, cry on, cry off, pain face, no pain face, make eye contact, no eye contact; no more picking up on ques to adjust my behaviour accordingly, I may even drop the polite manners. If I don't feel like smiling I won't, no more acting, it's such a relief after a lifetime.
The only concern I have is, do I trust myself?
I think I can, once I'm away from here and living a different life, doubting myself does not help anything but I know what I'm capable of; however, I'm not stupid, far from it, I wouldn't have got this far in life if I was.
I fooled police and courts, social workers and health visitors in the past. I convincingly rearranged the truth of many things; I succeeded in passing the buck on many occasions to save myself, not to deliberately hang another, it was simple survival instincts.
Like I said, when we were kids policies didn't exist, things weren't classed as abuse back then, neither was it abusing for the local bobby to smack you upside the head and drag you back home only to stand and watch you cop another one for being dragged home by the bobby.

Growing up I was fully aware there were different types of discipline and the discipline in our house was like no other that I knew of. Schools still caned pupils, teachers hit you with rulers and board rubbers were chucked at you; violence at home often meant violence at school too and on the street. You either feared the hand and cowered or you walked right into it and remained standing. Like I was told once " you're like a weeble, you wobble but you don't fall down" he was referring to my weight after he'd shoved me across the kitchen; but if you've learnt to take it as a kid, you take it always, unless there's no need, and for this past year, that has been the case.

The first year of my life that I have spent without flinching, ducking, defending, running, jumping, waiting, expecting, arguing, feeling sick, anxiously awaiting, nervous, dred, suspecting, being at beck and call, clearing up broken things, chucked meals, drinks, wine glasses, coffee cups, remote controls, ipads, macbook pieces, phone bits, hunting for sim cards in the mess, ripped clothes; no scrubbing carpets, well not for that reason anyway.
It's been peaceful on the whole, busy but all on my own terms.

They say it takes a full calendar year to recover from someone's passing, I recovered much quicker than that.

If you are wondering about the moral of this confessional story, there isn't one really, I'm all out of morals and no one from 1 Narcissist Road was particularly moralistic. Like I've said I can't blame my past for the actions I've taken, I co-created my environment as an adult so I cannot say that I killed him for being abusive, I allowed it to happen and to continue.
All I can say is, don't do as I have done, is that the moral?

Never in a million years would I have thought that I would be sitting here broadcasting events from narcissist road, family matters were private; but then I hadn't dreamt in a million years that I would have done what I did, and 3 times; I wouldn't have had to up and leave nor feel the need to wipe the slate clean. The only reason I'm telling you about narcissist road, is due to context and to make myself understood, this is what I did and why.

Let me remind you however, that I didn't act without justification; I was once of fractured mind, but I'm not now.

The fractured mind thought it was courage to stay the course, but it was in fact courage in ending it.

He got no more than he deserved and that's the fact of it; his head and heart are being taken care of in a fitting way, parts of him went into the sewer with the rest of the shit; some was consumed by his own dogs, some by rats, fox, and even ducks; the rest of him was scattered all across town, in dog poo bins, down with tommy and including with the wicker wolf.

It amused me as the story involves a decapitated head being taken off into the woods and was relevant to our wedding photos, of which went up in flames along with his particular body part and a dose of curse.There are a multitude of ways to cast a curse I have discovered; clearly some of these websites are fancied up to earn them money and things one reads has to be taken with a pinch of salt, in some cases witches alter salt! Those in the know tell you for free and like I've mentioned, many of these products have great aromas which overpower and neutralize the smells one doesn't wish to inhale. I've no intention of finding out what burning scrotum smells like, gross. It had to be done however, I doubt any creature would wish to consume that, nor would I inflict it upon them, that could be considered animal cruelty.

After much digging I found a site, it simply stated
'The Road Goes Ever On'.
I considered this a sign, in that indeed it does if you continue on it; I was stepping off it but wished him to remain on it forever, never reaching an end.
So I did as it said and chucked it all in with his parts along with a spectacular display of lycopodium flash dust fireball; which was actually a bit expensive and was obtained from outside this country so as not to draw attention of purchase. The wedding photos and his relevant body part went in an impressive display whilst I cursed his soul to walk that road for all eternity.
Whether this will be the case I will never know, whether the whole curse thing is nothing but hocus pocus matters not really, but I did get satisfaction and it was extremely good fun making fireballs and bursts like a mad magician stealing the show.
I had sort of done that before with flour, chucking flour onto a fire makes sparks and bursts, albeit small, it's mildly entertaining, so I thought I would go one step further and gave it a splendid display of a dark madness finale.

Getting to the wicker wolf was tricky, but it had to be done. I obtained scratches, stings and small cuts, my hair got caught up on foliage as did my coat; I wasn't able to take my dog through all that to get there, he would have been highly confused and uncomfortable. I tied him to the fence the other side near the stone resembling a giant birdbath, walked around the water and pushed myself in; twigs smacked me in the face and ripped at my hair, it was so quiet all I could hear was the snapping of the twigs under my feet and the shoosh shoosh of the reeds. It was weird, like they were telling me to be quiet and that they knew it was a secret. Shooooosh.

By the time I got to the wolf I was battered and my face was bleeding and my legs were stinging from those blasted huge nettles. I could then see my dog sitting there across the water, watching, listening like a little guardian. I didn't speak to him, I just did a thumbs up then a point down, whereby he laid down and silently waited whilst I dug under the running wolf and disposed.

Getting back out was easier as I had trodden much down but fully aware I was to obtain more stings and scratches. I got the dog's frisbee out of the backpack, put the backpack back on and waded back from whence I'd come, frisbee in hand in case of the unlikely event that someone was still here after closing. Although it closes anyone can walk into here if they wish, the car park closes to this massive ground but ways to enter by foot are many and in several parts; my excuse was going to be that my dog's frisbee went in there and although I tried to leave without it, look at him, that's as far as he would go, he's a bit obsessive, so there we are I've got it. But there was no one, not anywhere, so I put the frisbee back into the backpack before I went round to him as there really wasn't time to play.

It would soon be dark and I had one more disposal that day; we continued toward the arboretum, cut through the wood walk whereby he pretended to chase rabbits on the way and reached the fat Toad. Fat grotesque toad was easier to get to and I didn't have to leave him. Weirdly he was wary and started growling, backing off then going cautiously forward, then baking off and growling. At first I thought that there was someone back there, but I then realised he was reacting to fat toad; I laughed and went up to it and knocked on it and said, it's not real.

It took him a while to get close enough to sniff and realise it wasn't alive, he then cocked his leg and peed up it; fair enough, that's what I think too, I disposed in a puddle of urine soil and we left to play frisbee all the way down with no other person in sight, we passed by the banks of the wicker wolf and I smiled as the reeds said shoosh.

For some reason that clamering about in that thicket and the gooey ground under fat toad, made me remember geocaching; such a silly activity really.
I hadn't done it here, but I had some years ago whilst working abroad, trying to follow instructions and read clues in a foreighn language.
At the same time it was a fun way to explore the area but some finds were in some damn near dangerous places, which I guess was half the point of it all.

That day's disposals probably triggered those moments of memories as a few times were near misses; one of which involved climbing down a high bank into the estuary bed that involved tide dodging. The clue and find were in a chained and water tight container; anyway, to cut the long event short, you had to get down, find it, document it, prove it by tagging yourself, take a photo then get back up without being caught by the tide. It was the element of fear that caused the adrenaline rush, which made you stumble and make mistakes resulting in the climb back up being tricky business.

Another time involved not getting trapped on an island for hours when the tide came in, and it came in really fast, the causeway would be covered in no time; once I was caught crossing it back to the mainland with the dogs.

The little old dog who passed away last year and crossed the rainbow bridge to wait for us, she was petrified when the waters began to rise. She was shaking really badly despite the water being a trickle across the path, but when you stand still and look to your left and to your right, all you can see is the sea; for a moment as it covers the way it looks like you are walking on water.

Dogs have instincts, she knew the sea could engulf her, she asked to be picked up which I did, she shook the whole time, but the other dog, my faithful guardian of all dark deeds done, he attempted to swim which hindered the progress across.
It was somewhat of an adrenaline moment as the level hit my knees and he was still swimming, connected to the lead; attempting to swim to shore, that of which he wouldn't have made and neither would have we (me and older dog)
By the time the sea hit my thighs I scooped him up under my arm. One over my shoulder, one under my other arm, wading whilst killing myself laughing; no one was any the wiser that I had wet myself; partial excitement, partial fear and the hilarity of the situation caused by a dog who considered himself an olympic swimmer.

Hours before both dogs had been bombing around on exposed sands when the tide was out, chasing seagulls until they flew off, getting crabs from under rocks and eating them; not nice and neither was their poop after such activities. I had been getting clams and razor clams, have you ever done that with razor clams? Sprinkle a little salt in the sand where the air bubble is, and they pop up out of the sand, extraordinary.

Good moments, tainted by a temper fit and swift departure leaving me and the dogs to get back by ourselves (lucky there was a free bus in high season) temper fit as it was hot, hungry and bored.
The dogs were that good moment and sadly moments I will have to forget. But I won't need to scramble through thickets or climb down banks or into dirty waters or dig holes or any of the like again, so geocaching and adrenaline rushes shouldn't mind pop; out of sight out of mind, one hopes.
Relocating will have no relevance to the past, mind pops should cease shouldn't they, but there may be the option of the brain chip in the near future, a possible last resort, maybe.

If the road to hell is paved with good intentions, then the road to heaven would be paved with bad ones, therefore all roads have the potential to be paved with any intention; my intentions have benefitted the wider population in that there are 3 less mean people to inflict their bad intentions on all roads not just my road; this means I won't and don't have any guilt about it, therefore it should be easier to forget and go fourth on the road ahead having no intentions at all, just to go with the flow and enjoy whatever time I have left, the hard part is over.

I would like to have a small holding, big enough to have various animals, that's what I would like to have in my later years; feeding and looking after animals, a calm and content little place. But before that I would like to see some more of this marvelous world; but that will not be possible right now, not only do I have to ensure the wellbeing of my faithful friend and confidant, who deserves to live out the rest of his days in a place that's dog friendly and dog safe; which is where we are heading pretty soon.

But this 'pandemic' and those behind the scenes have other plans, so how much more of this planet that I will get to see and experience before I die is anyone's guess.

It will depend on who wins this war, if they have their way our experiences will be more virtual than physical and it will mean compliance; I've had enough of being compliant, at the time I finally break free I'm expected to tow the line again, but to someone else, and I don't even know them and never will, how mental is that.

Anyway, in the meantime it is my responsibility to ensure that my dog's retirement is enjoyable and that he is rewarded for his loyalty; even if he could speak I'm pretty certain he would never tell of our year of adventures, well he couldn't really could he, he would be admitting to being an accomplice and I am sure he was aware of what he ate. It would be a nice thought and to say that we will end our days together, but devastatingly, sadly, we won't. He is already getting on in years but he has had good adventures and there is still time to have more; I guess my intention now then is to ensure his road ahead is happy and full of fun, I will make sure he doesn't look back as we drive away.

They say that fact is stranger than fiction, I believe this to be true. If my grandmother had documented her dreadful life it would have read like a horror fiction, an unbelievable manufactured story; a senseless cruel tale of child abuse followed by domestic abuse, the stuff that nasty movies are made of.

I've seen the documentation of all her placements, all in the name of god and charity; I've seen both my grandparents shipping records, numbered like cargo. I've seen where the establishment wrote that she didn't fit well and her services were no longer required, each time she was removed and placed in another; she had eleven placements in the end. But none of it documents the abuse and exploitation of the child; I've read of the children that died in service and of those that killed themselves to end the misery and torture of those placements. These are all facts but one would think they're reading fiction.

What fiction cannot document is the 'inside knowledge' of the moments, they can only describe in the third person as they simply weren't really there. The facts that are stranger than fiction hold the key moments that make it real. A nanosecond, a split second, a long second which comes from being so stunned that you are caught in that moment and fail to notice what's happening after.
Like the hard thump in the stomach that's so hard that it winds you and the pain is so bad and overwhelming that after you've dropped to your knees, you are still stuck in that moment, you are still winded and stunned, you fail to notice that you've also been punched in the head after; you didn't notice at the time as you're still stuck in the previous moment.
When fiction writes that you are being dragged by your hair across the floor, they may write that your legs are getting carpet burns and that your heart is racing; fact would write that it feels like your heart has stopped beating and you have no breath, and the veins in your neck hurt and your windpipe is about to snap, all you can do to prevent the forthcoming attack is to try to grab out with one hand to fight or delay what's coming, whilst the other hand tries to pull your head back on. Though the fear cannot be expressed enough in words, fiction doesn't have the strange moments of fact; just like the time I felt bad for screwing up my dad's glasses after he had been vicious, he couldn't see without them and his squinting and him saying I can't see, made me sick to my stomach. Figure that one out!

He had been violent and lashed out at me for nothing that I had done, so I screwed up his glasses with gritted teeth; I was then filled with guilt and felt sad that he couldn't see.
A frying pan over his head would have been justified, but I felt guilt from taking his vision; a small strange fact but fact nonetheless.

Sometimes true stories sound so ridiculous that no one would believe them, so you don't tell them as you know you wouldn't be believed; you don't tell as you would be perceived to be a storyteller, an exaggerator, a liar. That is a true strange fact.
It is a bit insane that one would need to lie to be deemed trustworthy; human behaviour including my own is truly bizarre.

Books that I read eons ago like the jigsaw man and picking up the pieces and various other criminology and forensic literature tell of real life horror stories; I've also read real life files of those I've worked with, all facts, but they mostly lack reality of those moments that even the holder would have trouble expressing.
Moments are mainly images, it is difficult to write an image; for me it's the faces that express what words cannot. I've sat and listened to people relive what they did, (most was only the once, none 3 times) they describe it from the perspective of the victim, my guess is they were visualising the face that expressed the pain and fear, and like myself, this is what imprinted on my brain from childhood, the faces of my siblings and that of the perpetrator; it's difficult to write a facial expression.

As said, our family matters were private, but had I of chosen to tell any, I doubt I would have been completely believed as some of it sounds ridiculous despite it being the truth; likewise if I told people some of the things I had seen under the guise of care, it would seem unbelievable, as things like that don't happen, but I'm afraid they do.

Life can teach you much when it isn't in the realms of 'normality', this knowledge helped me achieve what I did 3 times and how to deal with it all appropriately, the stranger facts were easier to relate to than any fiction; strange facts were my reality, I found the rules easier to follow. Being clever in ways that aren't used in 'ordinary' lives, ways of the like minded, the stranger facts of the strangest folk.

This pandemic has made normal folk do strange things, like wearing a mask whilst exercising outside, driving their cars alone whilst wearing a mask, wearing a mask, a visor and exercising in the middle of a field; telling you off for not wearing a mask whilst walking your dog along a river bank where you are likely to meet more wildlife than humans; becoming so paranoid that they won't leave the house; yet no one acted like this during every winter being flu season.

Much of the time the flu vaccines are predicted incorrectly, as is well documented and you can't really predict a virus mutation. This has been shown with the pandemic, anyway every winter thousands succumb to the flu, nobody hid away or wore masks, but such was the propaganda normal folk behaved abnormally. (and some still do) Whilst I don't have a tv (in order to not have 'all kinds of everything') I did and do of course, have internet access; I did read of the goings on and occasionally listened to the news but I did not get sucked in on the propaganda, I did my research.

All information is out there, factual documents; there are other reasons the fear was and is hyped up. Locking everyone away was measured in the impact to the environment, look it up for yourselves. There is always more to things than you think, you should always question 'motives' take nothing at face value. If enough people had questioned, maybe the domino runway would have fallen in a different direction. But the vast majority watch tv and read the news papers and believe everything they read, despite the facts missing those important moments of reality that tells you it's real and a fact. Instead most people hung on every word of suited politicians with graphs and predictions. Normal people developed strangely entranced brains, I wasn't expecting that.

I wasn't expecting the situation to make my life easier as everyone was stuck in a trance focussed on something that the vast majority wouldn't even encounter.
Fear kept them transfixed and self focused, nobody noticed me, apart from mr brain tumor; services closed down, everyone went into their own cocoons, self absorbed with fear and survival.
Normal folk got sucked right in and literally hid away.
I had no visitors therefore didn't fall foul of the curtain twitching brigade, the spies wanting to pick up the phone to snitch on their neighbours, one almost transported back in time to nazi germany.
It wouldn't have gone amiss for people to have acted like those of that old movie 'the body snatchers' where they squeal and point out the real human being who had escaped being cloned.
The pointing finger to squeal on the neighbour for having a relative come by; stand back and analyse that, when you needed your family most, it was forbidden; divide and rule by fear, lonely people, scared people, being more susceptible to control.

Anyway, whilst all that was going on around me, I was busy dismembering and disposing in plain sight, unnoticed, invisible, aided by a strange happening that pretty much paralysed most.

Check on your loved ones by phone and media the news said, my phone didn't ring and I had no one to check on (although I could have opened the freezer for a chat)

I wasn't concerned that someone would come by; I was shocked to hell when she turned up unannounced, but dealt with that in a blink of an eye, thereafter I had no worry or concern.

People had been punched in the stomach, winded so bad that they remained in that moment for a very long pause; whilst I went about my private family business unobserved.

To this day no one has come by nor called, no doctors, no dentist, no nobody.

Good luck with your healthcare is all I can say as they still wouldn't notice if you're dead or alive; as i write this, over a year has passed and GP appointments, I've heard, are still only via phone.

I will be long gone before they get their act together and bother to take a look at their lists.

But I do feel bad for people that needed treatments and couldn't get it.

Thankfully I needed nothing and the cuts I gave myself accidentally didn't require stitches; I was very very careful as I had already considered that it would draw attention and how would I explain myself. I was very lucky that that hammer hadn't come down on my head, a stark warning to pay attention. I was very focussed and careful.

Chopping was easier than cutting, cutting took longer concentration; I did discover that rib bones splinter, that livers are actually heavy as are intestines, by far the worst and most unpleasant task. I did catch myself a couple of times noticing small scars and my mind fleetingly remembered how they came about, more so on him than her as she had left by the time she was 18.

She had had work done, her nose wasn't the one she left with and she had grown into a women, I only really knew her as a youth, I had little knowledge of most scars, probably the most striking thing that I fleetingly noticed was her teeth; I wasn't sure if they had grown back so brilliantly after they were knocked out when she fell one day running from her brother, or if she had had work done on those too. But I had to ignore these fleeting thoughts and concentrate on the task at hand. Like I said, I was careful with her head, the face was a work of art, I didn't ruin it.

I do have something to add here, whilst I've just thought about it, although she was the devil on two legs and I'm confident that given a different environment she would still have been the same; I did fail to protect when they were young, there's no excuse, it's no good me saying I didn't know any better and it's all I'd ever known.

I did know better, therefore I failed and the years slipped by.

Years that cannot be retrieved and rearranged; I do admit to bearing resemblance to my mothers actions in sweeping things under the carpet, it was my normal yes, but it shouldn't have been theirs. Maybe this will come back to get me, maybe it won't and whilst they didn't receive the type of violence I did, they witnessed what they shouldn't and were mentally tortured when I wasn't home; I did nothing to change that and looking back albeit briefly now, standing on the outside looking in, I didn't do what I should of, that is 100% fact.

The revenge that I took on him won't be known to them, the revenge doesn't benefit them as those little children don't exist.
The revenge is out of time and out of context for the little children who are fleeting ghosts in a mind pop. Too little too late.
Like a drone on a treadmill I trudged on blinkered with the attitude of stay the course.

I can't even call myself an optimistic victim, once an adult can you be a victim if there is an escape route?
As for optimism, what was I hoping or thinking would happen?
But there we are, strange behaviour of a strange person, which would be deemed normal here.

I could liken myself to the loyal flag waving people who worship royalty, do they too not realise that royalty doesn't care about them, only their actions in flag waving and the boost to their egos in being worshipped?
But for what, Stag hunting? Fox hunting? Pheasant shooting? Killing animals for sport is not to be worshiped.
Being worshipped for living incredibly long and privileged lives?
Receiving the best food and the best healthcare whilst half the nation stands in queues at food banks and waits on long waiting lists for healthcare?
The untouchable and unaccountable royals worshipped for reasons only known to the worshiper, on their own blinkered treadmill of life.
My apologies if I've offended those whose loyalties lay with royalty, it's your right of course, it just means I have the same right to my beliefs.

Loyalty that I knew was about keeping quiet, loyalty to a family unit of the deranged, loyalty to a marriage that was as toxic as the 60.5

million face masks rated FFP2 manufactured by a chinese company; Toxic in that they contained biomass graphene and inhaling their particles is toxic to the lungs causing respiratory issues, ironic no?

The same graphene in the so called vaccines, the gene therapy, the graphene containing gene therapy. The masks sent out to hospitals, pharmacies, medical centres in respect to the virus. Toxic. Scary.

The marriage was as toxic as he was poison, I knew it but ignored the facts; my m-field went from one madness to another and I straddled them all, spinning around in them like a mad marble smacking into those invisible force fields.

My new life will have a new m-field, tranquility, like floating on your back in warm seas with the sun on your face.
My only loyalty now is to the dog.
No more manipulation, exploitation, blaming, shaming, guilt tripping, no threats, no blackmail (is that politically correct? Sorry if not) no more being used, lied to and lied about, no negative emotions or feelings of inadequacy; I've proven I'm perfectly adequate, I've been adequate all my life, I have many skills.
I've dealt with thousands of situations and I'm still here.

I do feel empathy for others, but I'm not some altruistic martyr and I don't wish to be remembered, I hate public speaking and have always avoided being centre of attention, never wanted any recognition for anything, say it, do it, leave.

I'm not sure however, am I weak or am I strong? weak people don't fight back or deal with things but strong people plough on through regardless.

A weak person doesn't take a life, carve it up and serve it up, or do they? Hard to say isn't it, but weak people aren't ruthless and I was. Being weak would come down to self esteem no? There's nothing adrift with my self esteem, I never considered that I was a worthless jelly when melted, I didn't melt in adulthood though I'm sure I did in childhood. My normal was abnormal and I was aware, but as an adult I didn't think I was worthless.

I studied and used that knowledge and even fought the resistance to that knowledge, from him. I actually considered that I had a better understanding of abnormal behaviours, I lived it, so of course I did.

I had remorse despite this being uncommon in narcissist road, no one ever said sorry, I don't know if like me, they felt it but didn't show it and on thinking about it, I don't think I showed it either.

But I don't feel remorse for what I did last year, not any of it, that was all different to small acts of revenge.

Like I've said, that first time was not thought out prior, nor was the second and although the third was, it had nothing to do with family matters.

In some strange warped way I think I thought at times that I understood my fathers terrible behaviour; it is said that our subconscious knows the meaning of experiences even if consciously we do not.

Maybe that's why my small acts of revenge remained just that, as I had ample opportunity to end him in those latter years, but then again maybe the mental hold was ingrained.

Does it really matter anymore? Probably not, the past is almost at an end anyway.

No one has all the answers do they and not all behaviours fit into some tickbox or label; some behaviours would be seen as traits of various 'labelled' conditions, a bit like a headache being a symptom of various health conditions.

Sometimes it takes other symptoms at the same time for a diagnosis to be observed.

Behaviours on their own can be seen as a single entity / activity but if there are equal displays of other particular behaviours they then group them and label them as a whole.

Like the headache, a single behaviour can be just that, meaningless and harmless, it's just a headache, fred shouts a lot but he's harmless.

Patterns and frequency attract the labels, or so it is believed.

Should one act of self harm born out of a terrible situation in which a mind could not cope any other way, then gift you the label of self harmer, self injurer, no it shouldn't but it can. And depending on who is on duty at the time and the state of the mental health system, could see one put on section, from there on in one is at the mercy of the system.

Sometimes money is involved, sorry but it is true.

I worked at a private mental health hospital, all persons were on section for various reasons. Some clearly needed to be, some clearly did not; some were unfortunate enough to be in the wrong place at the wrong time. This particular hospital (for want of a better word) were paid massive amounts of money by local authorities across the country, to take 'overspill' from wards, hospitals, services and even bigger amounts for individuals with extremely challenging behaviour.

Depending on the section of the mental health act, the individual's behaviour, the risk, negotiated the pay package worth (the person's worth to the private hospital). I wasn't complaining at the time as I was being paid a fair amount of wage; however, after a while things began to play on my mind as I witnessed some people's lives go down the swanny.

Where there's money, there's manipulation; I witnessed people denied the release from section as they were worth too much money.

I sat in reviews and witnessed exaggerations of people's behaviours and risks by psychiatrists, psychologists, social workers, heads of nursing, in order to keep those people on section, to have them stay longer, another guaranteed six months of receiving the large payout from that local authority.

A robbing of funds into private hands and another ruined life.

Some people had displayed one act, one behaviour, mostly for a good reason but ended up in a system where they became so trapped and institutionalised, that they began picking up traits from others and formed patterns of behaviours as a coping mechanism, which then earned them a label of a particular condition.

These were learned behaviours from the environment, they weren't innate; had that person not been in that environment they would never have picked those traits up.

The longer they're in it, the more the display of behaviours, this includes withdrawal.

One doesn't need to be violent or loud or a risk to others, withdrawal (a normal response to such environments) can deem you a risk to yourself.

Allowing domestic violence can label you as a self harmer; a response or retaliation to something can deem you violent; it is all dodgy ground if you ask me.

Refusal to take medications can get your 'capacity' to decide taken away from you; I've witnessed forced medications and chemical cosh incidents many a time and most unjustified.

Shortages of staff for a shift meant the most tricky persons wouldn't take up staff time, the person would be subdued against their will the second they blinked wrong.
There were some 'professionals' who I considered serial cosh's, easy shift, easy life; sign this form as witness, double breaks.

I've seen staff with hangovers lean against doors for ages (sitting on the floor with their backs on the door) so the occupant couldn't come out. I've seen people put in seclusion, door locked, for bad mouthing, even though sometimes what they said was the truth.
Places like this have an abundance of behaviours to learn and even staff picked up traits. The difference being, staff went home after shift and were free to leave.

Does one act of self harm make you a self harmer, no, if you lash out in self defence does it make you prone to violence for the rest of your life, no, it doesn't.
If your insulin levels went wrong and you were momentarily aggressive, does that mean you will have a history of violence and be a risk, it shouldn't but it can.

If you take a life, justifiably, are you a murderer and a risk to society? Well that one has been debated for eons hasn't it.

Murder in self defence, 'manslaughter'; who makes these words up?

Look at the word narcissism, a myth about a handsome young man who fell in love with his own reflection; sometimes I think it is the professionals and systems that are actually the mad ones.
Psychopathy, translates as suffering of mind or soul.
Machiavellian, the end justifies the means...seems pretty logical that doesnt it.

Behaviours, we are all capable of the inappropriate ones, sometimes we are understood, sometimes we aren't; as previously stated what sets us all apart is frequency and duration.
What defines a serial killer?
Research says 3 or more kills, does that make me a serial killer? of course not.

Serial murders are relatively rare; I am pretty reclusive and live alone, the majority of serial killers are not and do not. Serial killers mostly do not appear as a 'strange person', whereas I am. For example, Yates who killed 17 sex workers, was middle class, army national gaurd, married with 5 children, an upstanding member of the community; he buried a victim in his yard under his bedroom window.

The Green River Killer (Ridgeway) killed 48 women over 20 years, kept his employment for over 30 years, was married and attended church, read the bible and spouted religion.
Rader, killed 10 people, employed by the government, ex air force, boy scout leader, married with children, president of his church.

Serial killers plan, have defined areas of operation, have motives; it is understood that serial killers suffer from a variety of personality disorders. Whereas, I had no plan, no motive and do not have a personality disorder, as you can clearly tell.

The first was spontaneous, the second I had no option, the third, although planned and with motive, was justified in all ways.
Firstly, that beast couldn't continue, secondly, he would have been caught at some point, drawing attention to these walls, I couldn't allow either.
So no, I'm not a serial killer. But a tickbox would say otherwise, do you see what I'm saying about that and how easy it is for some to become unfortunate victims of the system.

Real serial killers select, target, approach, control, kill, dispose. It is recognised that the logistics of the act and disposal can become very complex and further complicated when multiple sites are involved.

It is easy to recognise that the above is not all relevant to me; there was no selection and target, they were all within these walls; I didn't need to approach and control, they were all here and the first two were the ones who controlled, not me.
The beast was probably controlling to his victims, but I didn't have any control over him, which is why he had to cease.

The only logistics involved was disposal, and although none of it was easy peasy, it wasn't hard. Maybe you have to have a good memory for it not to be complex; maybe as I didn't have all the issues of the former mentioned list of tasks before I had a dead body to deal with, made it less complicated?

Multiple sites during a lockdown was far easier I'm sure, but also from what I had learned, multiple sites are more successful; but since I'm not a serial killer, I didn't have multiple bodies.

However, I will admit I did lax on the third and last, it is one site, but different locations. Like I've said, it took me all day but that's because the body was in multiple pieces.
Maybe most serial killers just kill and dispose of the body whole; but of course some do dismember.

On average this is because functionally it is easier to dispose of; clearly if I had of dug a deep grave in the back garden, dragged the bodies and chucked them in, I would have been seen wouldn't I. Likewise, how would I have gotten bodies bigger than myself out of the house and into a car without being observed, and then what would I do with them after, which would have ensured they would never be found? So obviously I was left with no option but to chop and cut them up; none of it was part of any big plan.
Not in a million years would I have dreamt of any of it, well not that I recall although smashing him in the face was probably a plan of the subconscious, the other me that I don't know much about consciously.
The precision in obtaining bullseye could have been considered well practiced, but then again as kids and youth we had played darts an enormous amount.
As mentioned, my dad was a good dart player and only recently did I get rid of all the trophies that sat all over the place for years until mum died. Quite why she left them in situ for all those years I've no idea, but they're gone now.

But anyway I guess one could say that I have very good hand eye coordination, which is probably responsible for successful first strikes, 3 times.

It must be down to learning coordination early in life; I was in fact very good at netball, goal attack was my position, I could and still can hit a ball with a bat, every time, I never miss. Maybe that skill was handed down to me along with everything else received here. Precision being the skill to carry out all kills, cuts, disposals adequately.

By the time I had to get rid of the beast I was well practiced and confident; it was the how and when that required planning. He was so private that I rarely saw him face to face. It wasn't the case that he would be sitting at the kitchen table eating or drinking and I could pass by, lift the doufeu and crack him over the head; he wouldn't be washing up where I could chuck an electrical item in and electrocute him.

I advertised the room as non intrusive and was very private myself; it was simple room lodging, no shared lounge, no socialising; so how to get close enough without being noticed actually took some thought.

I didn't know his patterns of in and out as he didn't really have any, sometimes he was gone all night, sometimes for a few days at a time. He was taller than me (not hard to be really) but not of big build; it would have been absurd to hide in an empty room and wait for him to come out, aside from the fact the floorboards creak and the doors squeak, the wait could have been hours.

The rent was paid by leaving the cash in the pot at the bottom of the stairs, getting close enough was not a normal happening like the other two.

I thought about obstructing the lock to the door so that he had to knock, but still he would be too tall and how would that get me behind him, it wouldn't, I would have been in front.

I thought about tripping the electric when he was in his room so that I could make him check where his electricals were plugged in, but it was very unlikely he would let me enter the room since he had things to hide.

I only knew he did as I had knocked the cctv camera sideways accidentally when cutting the climber from the phone line. There were 4 cameras at the front of the house; I took the top two down after I had dealt with him. I didn't even realise that they could move from side to side, I hadn't installed the cctv and cameras, he had some years ago, after he fell out with someone and became paranoid that they were ruining his precious car.

I took no notice of the cctv normally; only during lockdown and whilst handling the family matters did I have them on but otherwise usually the screens were off.

I had to get the creeper off the phone wire, this creeper is a blinking nightmare and was and still is, getting out of control. I'd no idea the camera had swung or indeed how long it had been that way.

There was an argument out here in the road one night, I couldn't see as it was dark, if I'd pulled the curtains the light would have shone out, before you know it I would have been involved or accused of snooping.

So I used the cctv; as I flicked through the 4 camera screens I got a terrible shock.

Initially I was confused as to what on earth I was looking at, then I realised I was looking into the side of the front upstairs room, the net curtain made it a bit fuzzy but I was looking at the tall stand dress mirror, what was reflecting in it was a computer monitor, it was what was on the screen that stunned me.

I turned the cctv screen off, I felt really sick and ill, heart palpitations and broke into a nauseous sweat, I did not sleep that night. Many things fell into place about that lodger and I knew what had to be done, sooner rather than later.

That is how I found out, otherwise I would not have known.

If I had never found out, it is possible that attention would have been drawn to this house and I would have been very unprepared.

That is why he had to go, but not onward so that at some point he would have been traced back to here.

After the deliberations of how, I concluded, keep it simple and in plain sight.

I opened the loft when he was out, put the boxes on the landing, one of which I put to the side and open, containing the doufeu, in plain sight. I left the loft open, I left the boxes, he came back in and couldn't get to his room, blocked by the boxes and ladder.

I came out of my room and said oops sorry, I got exhausted putting a load of stuff up, I took a break, I'll move them.

I went up stairs, he stepped aside, I picked up the doufeu and looked up to the loft, then said, it'd be quicker if you gave us a hand, can you just chuck some up there?

He didn't speak, bent down to get one, put it up, bent down to get another and I struck, just the once, it was enough.

I had considered there's a 1 in 4 chance, just like genetics, that he would be in the right position at the right time. But it turned out much quicker and far easier; he went down on the first blow, I did 2 more to ensure.

He was on the landing, a spit to the bathroom.

No elaborate staging, he saw the doufeu but it had no significance or meaning, just like the other junk in the boxes from the loft.

Chopping and cutting him up was far quicker and easier; he was thin plus I had obtained a new knife for her, sharper and lighter. For him, the first, I didn't care that the cutting was raggedy, I simply needed to dispose of him.

I had obtained a Japanese chef's knife, the yoshihiro gyutou, stain resistant blade made of vg-10 hammered damascus stainless steel; it is recommended as it is said to 'rock through meat' (which it does) and it has a blade cover for storage.

It was on the expensive side but my dad always said "you're only as good as your tools" meaning bad tools, bad job. I had to agree on that as I discovered the first time, although the meat cleaver and butcher's box served extremely well; I couldn't have achieved any of it without the meat cleaver, his payment in kind from all those years ago.

If he had had a crystal ball he wouldn't have bought that back home would he; what he should have done, had he had any intelligence, was to have sold it and bought the money back home. For one it would have made his lie look more believable, for two, it wouldn't have come back at him years down the line, why did he even keep it one wonders. Some warped satisfaction to the ego every time he came across it? whatever, it actually came across him in the end, many times.

I can't say that he was a textbook narcissist as his behaviours crossed over and ticked boxes for the other two traits of the dark triad.

Relationships with these people are exhausting and draining, literally every day brings a challenge in some form or another; their brains, his brain, worked differently with a horrible mean streak.

Over the years I did work with some of these types but they appeared far more intelligent than he, as was she. She was different to him in most ways, far more calculating, far more untrustworthy, would cut you down and hang you out to dry for what would seem no apparent reason.

He lacked intelligence to be what he wanted and his coping mechanism was violence and destruction. The marriage was hard work to say the least; he took offence at the drop of a hat and caused repeated arguments until the cows came home; sometimes the intention was to genuinely cause harm and not just to me.

If you recognise any of this, you have a choice to stay or go; ask yourself is this it for the rest of my life?

If you think that at some point they will change, you are wrong, they won't.

They may get weaker with age, their ability to perform physical abuse may decline but they won't change, they are wired that way. They will never see you in a better light nor will they love you more, they aren't capable, sorry.

Stop and think, will this rollercoaster eventually make me sick?

Agreed that the good times do seem exciting, but it all sours and everything good will be tainted; you will come accustomed to this and live for those momentary good times, it isn't acceptable and it isn't normal. It will get to you in the end.

Until you are out of it, you won't see the mess that it really is, they don't value you, if they did they wouldn't do and say those horrible things.

These people only view others as usefulness and worth, you are as worthy as the amount they can take from you. Give them everything and for a while they will be appeased, at some point it won't be enough, your worth will drop and they will focus on your flawed human qualities, at which point you will become a target.

Everything and anything will be your fault, they will blame you even for the imaginary.

You won't understand at first as to what is happening, this will cause confusion, which in turn will make you feel desperate and make you feel that you've lost control, the truth is, you have.

Narcissists have antennas to assess if they are perceived as special, worshipped, loved, respected; if any of that is not being detected it offends them, they don't appreciate that.

If they are not the centre of your attention and you are not giving your all to them, you are disrespecting their worth; roll out that red carpet or else.

In their defense of the assault to their ego, they will attack; they have no empathy so don't expect them to say sorry.

If they are not your focus when they require it, to avoid such attacks, the constant attention to detail and worshipping, will eventually wipe you out of energy leaving nothing left to maintain yourself.

Letting yourself go will also disrespect them, this is not what they signed up for, you cannot win; just a thought but, do yourself a favour, focus on yourself, not them, get yourself clean away.

Say to yourself, 'no more situations', rid yourself of those who depend upon 'external validation'; it's exhausting and will zap the life right out of you until there's nothing left to give anyway.

No constant validation means they aren't getting what they want; this is where they will betray you, cheat, lie and attack you. Imaginary happenings to accuse you, of which will drive you insane as you try to defend yourself against something that had never even happened. You will question yourself, your memory and your sanity; this tactic is that very purpose, beware the bizarre fiction.

They will be incredibly cruel and nasty and things will be used out of context as they deem everything about you reflects something that you didn't do yesterday. It becomes about the entirety of you, the relationship, the situations of today and the day after, that of which hasn't actually happened yet.

Truth twisting, furious moments where their hatred and despise is seen in their eyes and in their actions toward you, the surroundings and themselves.
I have no doubt that you know exactly what I'm talking about, would you read this otherwise?

Unfractured people wouldn't grasp any of what I've written, and why would they; unless you've encountered the 'constant victim' trait of the narcissist, the above situations would be unbelievable and senseless.

The fact is, ironically, they use fiction in their own victim scenarios. They see themselves as victims when their beliefs of their 'exaggerated' self worth is not recognised, in that things aren't working out as they should; it's not fair, poor me, none of this is my doing, look what has happened to me....because of you.

Work, home, social, wherever it goes wrong will always be someone else's fault and they will constantly be the victim, even their own abuse to others will be the fault of that person, they made them do it. The tiniest of disagreements become major events, it is just exhausting. Many people on the receiving end of the narcissist, end up with anxiety, depression, mental breakdowns, paranoia, delusions, diminished capacity to function and jumpy.

Due to narcissist road's upbringing, I got none of the above but I did on occasions drown myself in several bottles of wine, this I realise now was toward the end of my tolerance and the road toward me ending it all.

I did several things in those latter years actually but it was put down to menopause, I kid you not. The change of life was responsible for my retaliation, not me, a hormonal imbalance!

Narcissists are primed to be abusive, they simply don't care, they refuse to process a situation that has caused harm to someone else, basically they are incredibly selfish, with 'acted out' displays of generosity and sincerity; behind every one of these acts is a selfish motive. You simply cannot ever trust a narcissist, so if you are dealing with one, or two or indeed a family, it would be in your own interest to break free and never look back.

Don't leave it so long that you develop one or more of the aforementioned or worse and end up doing what I did. It is unlikely that you would accomplish what I did, you would highly likely be caught.

The warning signs that you are losing it and your coping mechanisms have been worn out, would manifest in various ways; you may not necessarily realise what is happening, indeed you too may be labelled as menopausal and actually believe that to be responsible. But at the end of the day, it's your life and your choice, just as it was mine; you, like me, are the co-creator and conscious cooperator, you are ultimately responsible for yourself, as am I.

I grew up in a family where responsibility for terrible behaviour was never taken, no one ever said sorry, like we were supposed to understand that you just accept and carry on.
I should have known better than to marry into something so similar to my environment, I've no excuse, it wasn't as if I wasn't familiar with those characteristics.

It is said that you rarely meet a narcissist who doesn't claim to have had a hard life, a difficult upbring; blaming this initially for any disturbing behaviour… "it's because my mother hated me" "my father is the reason I am who I am" "my ex-partner was an addict" and so on.
The blame is never theirs.

If I had not have done what I did, I would not be writing this and I certainly would not be broadcasting my life nor the happenings within it. I spent my entire life being committed to hiding the truth and facts, it had absolutely nothing to do with anyone else.
But I guess I was also ashamed and sat on the fringe of social life being careful to not let anyone in; getting in would mean they knew and if they knew, I would be viewed in a different way, and I didn't want to be perceived as a victim when young and as an idiot in adulthood, as lets be honest, no one in their right mind would have carried on in that relationship; as always, silence was what I hid behind.
The silence that proves I am not like them.

But it doesn't matter now who reads this and what they think, no one will ever know who I am anyway; but I will have wiped the slate clean, the truth setting me free.

If you wish to insult a narcissist, don't pat them on the back and praise them every five minutes; don't praise them for simply being a normal decent person, just don't be grateful every time they blink or enter the room, that should do it.
Be careful there though, there's nothing like an insulted narcissist, they will either flee or you will receive their wrath.
If they flee it will be because you are crazy, deranged, an addict or an abuser; a tarnished reputation is better than a ruined life, you can also correct the accusations, it's better if they do flee, however, they will more than likely be back.

Here is a warning, stated many times in the literature; in the early days of a relationship the narcissist will 'love bomb' their victims (yes victims) with attention and affection whilst pretending to be the best person in the world.
It is only when they are sure that they have hooked their partner that their true self starts to come through, the amount of time before it becomes an abusive relationship depends on the speed of the partner becoming hooked; then before you know it there's a 'trauma bond'.

It is also not uncommon for narcissists to fake illness and conditions to 'guilt trap' partners, from this they can exploit, it doesn't matter to them if it doesn't work out in their favour, they simply move on; but that is only in the early days, once a partner is hooked it is already too late, bad experiences will inevitably follow.

On a note, if you recognise any of the above, It is thought that the best revenge one can take is to get away, stay away and live your life to the full. You don't necessarily need to kill them.

My grandmother (dad's mum) really did have a terrible life, it didn't turn her into a narcissist, but I do believe she married one; she didn't have to, but she may have done so to escape service, and who knows, she may have been viewed as an easy target to hook, she was already abused and exploited.

My mother married my dad, I wonder if he hooked her before displaying those behaviours?
I married one and to this day I couldn't tell you if I got hooked, but I was fed a sad tale of woe that I fell for, hook, line and sinker; which later transpired to be full of untruths.

All of us did not 'need' to get married, all offsprings came later. What did we all have in common? Prior to marriage, we all had experience of violence, betrayal, mistrust and let downs, being our 'normality'.
The span of a good 85 years saw three generations of women experience wrong doings from cradle to, and through marriage; those two went from cradle to grave stuck in it, I have broken that chain, I won't be going to my grave stuck in it.
I say three generations over 85 years, but in fact if you include the spawn of satan, who did experience some of the above in childhood, then really it is four generations. The fact that she turned out the way she did, meant that she didn't stick around. But she did marry, although I cannot say if he was the same as the rest as I never knew him. But like I said, he was much older than her, he may have been controlling but I doubt she would have let him win.

So I guess 4 generations, spanning over 100 years, saw 4 women experience the very abnormal, and I'm only referring to the immediate bloodline.

Nothing had improved in a hundred years, welcome to Narcissist Road !

I cannot even say with complete certainty if the cycle is in fact now at an end, as somewhere out there the last person from within these walls is going about his life.

Yes he did take that quantum leap and cut all ties that bind, but I've no idea how he turned out. Is he 'normal' ?

Or has he merely relocated all the dark traits from within these walls? Has he married? How does he conduct himself?

Is he a narcissist, does he display characteristics of the dark triad? I will never know, I can only assume from the knowledge I hold of him before he got up and walked away.

He was on the whole a quiet person, he disliked attention, he wasn't a loner but preferred one or two friends as opposed to a group. He never started fights or arguments but could be pushed to retaliation. He loved animals and nature but was also tech smart.

As he grew he detached himself from any daily family life and spent hours in his room learning to program and building hardware; extremely intelligent, the older generation of this so-called family used to say 'he's been here before'.

He disliked cruelty and injustice; wasn't an attention seeker, on the whole mild mannered but when he blew he blew. In the latter years he didn't hide the fact that he hated his sister and father; he once ripped his bedroom door off its hinges and chucked it down the stairs at his fleeing sister in an attempt, as he stated at the time "to fuc.ing kill her".

My assumption is, he was smart and brave, quantum leapt into a 'normal' life and hasn't looked back. However, he did experience what no child should and the genes run through his veins and sit in his cells, but maybe mine and his great grandmother's dominate over those of the bad; so although I cannot state with certainty that it is all now at an end, I think I can safely say that after 100 years, when I close the door behind me and drive away, that it will finally be at an end.

The twist in the tale of this past year's pandemic is, when you all lost control over your lives, I gained control over mine.
Your lockdown gave me my freedom.
It is completely true that fact is stranger than fiction.
Am I concerned of what the future may bring? A little I guess, it's the unknown, who isn't wary of the unknown.
But not only has my micro life changed (for the better of course) but wider life has changed too; nothing will be easy from here on in and there are harder times ahead.

Like I've said, it's now or never, pretty soon there will be ways and means of keeping track of people, their / your / my movements, spending, financial status, social habits, health status, well everything actually.

So of course the fact that everything has changed has made for a sense of uncertainty.
For all we know we could be locked down again by winter, no matter the country we are in. As long as I'm gone from here by then, I guess I would learn to cope with a lockdown anywhere.

I would prefer however, for there to never be another lockdown, who wouldn't. A further lockdown would hinder my progress and make relocation inhibiting; I wouldn't get the chance to blend in and establish myself, I don't think I'm concerned with being isolated or lonely, I've spent all this time by myself.

I am aware that my social skills have diminished and that I've avoided eye contact for over a year, so communicating may feel awkward to begin with. It's a fact that it's human nature to avoid eye contact with people that you don't wish to engage with, as it's acknowledged to be an invitation to converse; obviously I didn't want to converse with anyone while out on family business. I didn't and don't want to converse when the aim was and is, to be invisible.
It may be tricky making eye contact again; I'm sure that sounds an odd thing to be concerned about, but **the last time I looked anyone in the eye, they were dead.**

I'm also apprehensive about my passport, I no longer bear much resemblance to the middle aged women in the photo, mentally or physically, my face has fell off.
What if there's an issue and it's questioned?

I had contemplated sending it off with an updated photo but considered the potential issues of it being held up in a backlog, being rejected and what if I needed to have the photo verified? Also would it draw attention or raise suspicion; at the end of the day I concluded it wasn't worth it. I'm sure it will be fine, many people lose weight and most of us age.

There is also of course an element of fear of being found out, even though I'm 99.9% sure I won't be; it's probably due to the anticipation of actually leaving.

The long awaited flight that you just want over, the pending dentist appointment that you want ended before it's begun; nobody likes waiting do they, but this wait has been a very long time, my whole life.

Before I go I will walk the town with my dog one last time; it will take from dawn to dusk, we will need the backpack for the day's supplies. One last sweep of the locations; a final farewell of the past life.

I won't be going back to that last location, there's no need. It's of no significance.

As I pass by La Volonte De Dieu and walk over the heart of stone, I will leave a plant that I've been growing. Lavandula Stoechas 'Victory', the plant's meaning is simple.. 'I won'.

The plant doesn't need to last, I'm content with a nine day wonder; fitting for the vicinity.

The farewell sweep will be just that, I cannot go directly onto or into every place; some are no longer possible, most will be long gone now and I've no wish to view what hasn't.

Neither do I wish to get wet, muddy, cut, scratched, stung or bitten ever again.

I won't be going directly to the singing ringing tree either, I've no wish to conjure up any visions; I had a nightmare once not long after I had performed her sacrifice; that it engulfed her heart and the tree was pulsating, dumdum...dumdum...like a heartbeat.

I cannot even begin to imagine a machiavellian singing ringing tree thriving on schadenfreude, or is that not why I was afraid of it to begin with?

With each location I will acknowledge the control is now mine to keep, and the memories will erase behind us as we walk toward the end of that road and finally step off.

From this house on the hill, number 1 Narcissist Road, we will take the longest walk we've done thus far.

As we pass by it will make all those moments in time become meaningless, the only way to let go of the past; the intention to forget is the only way forward. I cannot remember the good times without remembering the bad, any memory means I've not broken free.

Our walk will wipe out all things seen and done, wiping the slate clean means erasing everything.

One wonders how it will be possible to bury your past, everything you were, everything you've known which has made and reinforced the neuronal pathways of your being.

But they are just that aren't they, footprints formed by neurons firing, footprints on the brain; people who have bad memories have faulty neurons, they don't keep the dots connected.

However, if those with dark triad traits can conveniently forget or not acknowledge or suppress their dark deeds, then it is possible to choose to forget, closing down the neuronal pathways and make new ones by reinforcing them; this is how we learn.

If I have a really good memory, which I do even for small details, then my brain is good at retaining, meaning pathways in the brain work really well, in that my neurons talk to each other a lot. Given that fact, they can be trained to think differently, it isn't impossible, CBT is successful (Cognitive Behavioural Therapy) but not for those from the dark triad, their brains are wired differently.

I worked in an establishment that attempted CBT, based on the token economy as the program; it didn't go well, it was pretty much a disaster, showing such people cannot change the way they think, they are inherently selfish with undesirable behaviours.

For me to forget the whole of my life thus far lived, doesn't make me a narcissist, there's a difference between need and want; I need to move on as I don't want to get caught, I need to forget as I want a chance at a better life, I need to write all of this as I want to tell the truth. And anyway, they say home is where the heart is and I don't really have a heart, I don't really know what love is, but I think I must love my dog.

What are relationships anyway? Familiarity, comfort zones (control zones), financial security, back up, safety in numbers, someone to talk to, laugh with, go places with;
all participants are interchangeable.

Life goes on when people die or leave, love isn't necessarily required is it. Everything in life is temporary, nothing lasts forever; I don't want this house anymore and I don't need to have a heart. Not to mention that our lives are changing in ways far beyond what the average person is aware of and we won't really have control for much longer.

I don't have nor want material possessions, only that of which is necessary to get through life; I would rather do, experience and feel, go and see and appreciate. There is much of this world that I haven't experienced; much I don't know and I'm more than willing to learn. But I don't really know how far I'm going to get, the only sure thing is that I will have achieved getting off this island. (future data colony)

As I've said, if it hadn't been for the restrictions, I wouldn't have gotten this far. But in all honesty, as much as I hope and wish, there is no telling how much further I will actually get.
Things are moving much quicker than many thought they would. Countries are beginning to close their borders again and travelling without proof of vaccination, and the right kind of vaccination is moving closer with speed.
The New World Order are shutting the doors sooner than expected; I fear that it won't be long before all movement ceases.
Restrictions began with a virus running around the world; restrictions will continue because of it, but the climate issues will begin to play a bigger part.

As said earlier, many many things are going to change, much more than the changes thus far; the speed at which things are happening makes me anxious; and I have nerves of steel.
I am not really certain where I will actually be when it happens.
Of course they will give the population a chance to 'go home', to return to where they are meant to be living, but it may pose a problem for the likes of us, those heading elsewhere, the escaping.
I am hoping to be established somewhere before the above occurs, but realise time may be running out.

Besides all that, I don't want to experience things virtually, I want to experience them for real; I don't know what your thoughts are on this fast moving climate crisis, or your thoughts and knowledge on weather manipulation and on weather warfare, but I do have my suspicions that all this is tied up together, in order to implement the agendas.

If the planet were in crisis why would the elite be jetting about and sending rockets into space?
Why would they have allowed mining for bitcoin, which has made the wealthy wealthier?
Why would there be plans for power stations in particular countries? (And do read up on The Belt & Road Initiative)

Why do they allow the continued manufacture of plastic that has ruined the oceans and why would they encourage the manufacture of masks, of which are toxic when they are burnt and litter most corners of the planet.
Nothing makes sense where there's double standards involved.

Propaganda makes truth and lies indistinguishable, but that is the aim is it not, to confuse us and divide us and set one against the other. **Divide and rule** is as old as ever but still as effective. The constant barrage of bad news could send the most sane insane; as I've said, I don't have tv and am not brainwashed, but I do read. Looking at things from several angles of an argument can be just as confusing; but when large powerful organisations publish what they are about to do, then one comes to the conclusion that it's obviously true.

I am not sure about the climate crisis, but if it is true then there is a huge amount of hypocrisy going on, the wealthy and influential can't be dictating on what is ruining the planet (us) when they jet off, gain massively financially and live far more polluting lifestyles than the rest of us.

These same elite, same wealthy influentials, technocrats, benefitted massively in wealth during this pandemic.

The monetary gain in pharmaceuticals alone would feed the poor of this world; So one ends up questioning, through **reasoning and logic**, if this is all actually factual.

Indeed there are scientists who disagree but they are little heard and suppressed.

What I am sure about is the **technological takeover**, but a huge amount of people don't, can't, won't see what is coming. They think it is futuristic talk, they don't bother to read what is freely available including on their own government websites.

It is very much happening, it is in full swing; for good or bad, I don't believe there will be an escape. People are talking about going off grid, but that would require isolated communities which would need to supply healthcare and clean water to even begin with.

So being aware of what is happening and what is coming only allows for small preparation, it doesn't change it; being aware doesn't get you out of it, unless of course you own one of the bunkers in new zealand with loads of land.

Why did the elite buy the land and build the bunkers?

War? If so, with whom?

To be self-sufficient? If so, why?

Whatever it is, whatever is going on, whatever is going to happen, the fact is, I have gained.

Unwittingly the controllers, this New World Order, collaborated with me, they sent me lockdown, where I achieved what I otherwise wouldn't have.

Their control gave me control; but for how long I will keep control is out of my control.

I am expecting far worse to come, I can only try to get by and take each day as it comes; I'm hoping to still be alive in 2025, I will be 60. Will I have seen more of the world by then? Probably not much, unfortunately.

But do I even deserve to, considering?

THE FINAL FAREWELL SWEEP
THROUGH THIS QUAINT MARKET TOWN:

And so, to finish what I started:

Our final sweep of the town will take in the two long rivers which run through the town and meet in the middle, 8000 year old birds that run off to be cleaned miles away.
We will cross back and forth many times; that of which we will begin by picking the smaller one up at the bottom of narcissist road; watching out for the old bobby.

Turning right we will walk straight along the bank, minding out for the rats and at the third bridge heading out of town we will head for the woods; but there's no festival here.
Passing the dog poop bins that I used many times along the way.

We will then jump the river, or walk through the ditch, depending on if there's water or not, but if they've opened the gates up stream and there's too much water we will have to walk the long way round and double back, to pick up the woods bordering the fields and walk all the way up, passing houses, education and possibly horses as we go.

When we reach the top we will jump down (literally) into where there is a 'serious injury from falling'.
We will pass by above the bats who will be sleeping, minding our footing; there is no need to go down, you can't see anything.

Continuing through where my little dog may be lucky enough to see squirrels and rabbits to bark at, giving him a bit of fun on this marathon.
Then out the other side, ignoring the visitors, to the road with no path.

Turning right then next left across the road, we will plod up the lane that years ago was frequented by nomadic persons. You can't see much from here, just fields either side and it is a bit dodgy with the traffic; cars have to use passing places and not many people actually walk along here.

Then turning left, then first right, continuing down country lanes with no pavements, passing by all the ailing people.
To the place that went from medicine and botany to camping, but not for pleasure or leisure.

We will head for the pond where the ducks await their feed; from here we will look down on the view and observe the very old and very new; depending on the wind direction one may hear the time as well as just about see it.

It is an odd view and in my opinion, the elegance of the old has been blighted by the new and the view is ruined by industry. But the town has thrived on the two main ugly sights for many many years; both now associated with effects on the body, highs and lows.
We will be pretty tired at this point and may take a rest on the strategically placed tree before heading off on the long walk by taking the way of the king, heading out the back into open fields.
Heading left, the walk is long and exposed to the elements, the day will have to be chosen with the weather in mind.

From experience gained, if it is wet, there is no shelter, if it is windy there is no shield, if it is too hot our heads will know about it.
A trudging walk on the edge of the growing crops, bad on the ankles, it's very uneven; until we reach the big jump down, sliding is better to be honest, getting up the other side is tricky, there is nothing to grab hold of to pull yourself up and if it has water in it (not usually) one will get wet. It's not a great experience but there's no way over unless one walks miles on and I've no wish to bump into any hikers.

Once over, turning left, we will pass by the ditch with the grill where perfection lies.
Past the old barn, around the field on the inside, past where children play monday to friday, into the small woods with large holes in the ground, left by badgers that may have moved on. I don't know what badgers eat, but they may have had a feast.
From here one can view the steeple on the hill, it looks so quaint.

A thought just crossed my mind, either there are many religious buildings around here, or I subconsciously disposed within view of one, a weird but true observation.

We will then cross the field to the lane where I've never seen any of it's name, only sheep and thus far we haven't been pricked.

Crossing the road avoiding the gatekeeper, into the large grounds; it will be a long walk around here, the locations are many.
We will pass by ducks 3 times; the wicker wolf, fat toad, the object with no rights to territories; past where people can't find their way out and past where one could be baptised. We may stop to feed the animals but not all can eat what they are given.

We will walk through the vast amount of woodland areas with rabbit warrens, thickets and brambles, holes in the ground, sunken water holes, in the direction of an arboretum.
Here we will have to take a significant rest for sure.

Then we will exit at the other end, out onto the road, straight down, being careful that we don't get bowled over as we pass by; heading for the south gate, at the roundabout we will go to the beach.
Taking the single track all the way down to the beer sludge waters. Passing by the overgrown hedge rows, broken trees, stinking stale waters where fairly heavy objects can float, broken fences, prickly bushes, overhanging branches, stinging nettles, trees with faces, the green triangle; carefully crossing ten thousand men, but we won't be marching. I wonder how long those staples held up? I won't be going over and in to find out what he looks like now, no more drunken nastiness for me.

Then at the divided path we will hang a left turn to go up and over the road, to the path (liable to flooding) that may or maynot be under water that day; if it is we will have to go further down to take the path that only sometimes is impassable, in order to double back onto it, in order to pass by as intended. Then onwards, going through the waste land water area where long legged birds have taken up possession, along with floating garbage; passing by sheep that used to be horses. Many years ago the horses here used to pack a punch.
Doubling back across the road, back past the no overnight camping area, past the sunken fence and the redundant 'keep out' sign, to the path that takes you up the old lane of the brothers.

At the top we will turn right and walk until we reach the building of pretenders, the last in this county; opposite the building of depressing escapism.
Continuing down the old road where the smells are dictated by the process; crossing over the top of where bees once gave, to the old iron gate.

Through the gate, not forgetting to close it, the muntjac and running dogs could run out onto the road.
Up the grass bank path, passing Mary-ann, turning right, to walk over the heart of stone and leave victory in our wake, leaning on the stone of sacrifice, turning round to scrape my shoes then laugh as I walk past 'how a wife should be'.

We will then continue through the old grounds, zigzagging through the old stones, passing skulls and crossbones as we go; passing the empty walls, where did the contents go? we will walk with ghosts, religion and old justice. I will say goodbye to my grandmother, who unofficially walks the grounds whilst keeping family matters private and family secrets safe.

Going on through to the medieval grounds where we will visit the ducks at the closed entrance; chasing squirrels, dodging people, passing the big book; then walk over to cross rat bridge at the dead end (which will be open of course)

Turning right (not left, no time for games) to pick up one of the 5 ways in.
Passing by my unobservable vantage point where 'no man' likes to tread after dark.

It's a long walk from here and we will need to rest first and wait for two chimes of the Westminster clock; which we left behind when I scraped my shoes.

Sad in a way, but I won't hear again.

It has been my time keeper and my compass during my changing and challenging time.

A comfort on one hand, a sense of security, but an indication of time ticking away on the other.

After our rest we will then follow the river one way, passing thickets, gooey ditches and fields, the river to our left and the river to our right, crossing inlets and outlets where flooding does occur. The flooding here gives rise to all manner of floating and non floating things, it takes a long time to recede, only the land and wildlife knows what's passed through here.

We will head to the point where they jump on each other for fun; to go around, in order to cross over to follow the river back again, but on the other side, passing by thickets, drains and large fields, until we stop to ascend up and over the pollution.

At the top, turning right (but not looking left as I don't wish to see the SRT) in order to walk down, to visit the woods at the dead end road where traffic still flows.

From the dead end road, we will ascend to where acres are twice five, chasing rabbits as we go (he never catches anything, he is always on his lead) From here one can view the steeples below and realise one is now pretty much half way done.

Then we will cut through the woods, coming out at the fit and active, walking under the crows, to the road, to cross over to where they talk a lot, and from where one can view the entire town below.

We will appreciate how far we have walked and just how far we have come in this year or so; after a rest we will continue on down through the path of the thickets, where the humming is constant, then out the bottom where my old dog will 'shake' off all the foliage.

Knowing what's ahead from here I will cast my mind elsewhere and give the SRT a wide berth, sticking to the lane instead, we will walk up, not looking right. If I'm lucky the air may smell of candy floss though that is very unlikely.

Back at the top, we'll cross back over the fumes, having observed the steeples down below for the last time. We will walk on down, turning right through the gate of private land.

Passing old education, cutting through the built up area where monks once tread; over the bridge, crossing the road. Going on through the town from the gates of the east to the gates of the north, where we will continue walking until we feel like spring; avoiding any stray arrows from bows. Cutting through to the field and rivers, where we will have our last rest.

I doubt there will be any ducks as by now the sun will be going down in front of us.

We'll then continue on to walk the path that butts the train line where vast thickets grow, full of rubbish blown in and across from the speed above. Fenced by high railings, rubbish galore and the overgrown of the overgrown, untouched, unsightly, unreachable area.

Coming out we will head left to the woods of war, then cut straight up toward the gates of the west to catch the graveyard just before closing.

We will pass by Tommy and say farewell to all those that we are to leave behind here.Many years have passed, everyone has gone, the ties that bind are no more.

When I stand at my grandmother's grave for the last time, I will tell her she was the bravest person I've ever known, but I will question, was my role model unwittingly my hinderer?

Nevertheless, whatever there is of my so-called heart, I will leave it here, with her.

We will leave the gates, they will close behind us and we will return to 1 Narcissist Road and prepare for our departure.

As I write, right on cue of Saturn retrograde, I'm leaving the past behind to find something better. The unfinished business is finished; I've confronted the past, taken responsibility and have now taken the opportunity to start afresh.

I've wiped the slate clean by telling you, that of which was on a 'need to know basis'.

I've admitted to what I did, it's out there now. I hope that you wish me well as I tread into unknown territory, on my own.

As ducky from the land before time says "I am all alone I am".

Maybe I will be for the rest of my life, maybe not; unless I try I will never know.

I wish you good luck in your futures.
But take heed of what I've told you,
Live your life on purpose while you still can.
All the best.

Sit on the throne of judgment
And judge all those below
But know it's not your purpose
Some things you do not know

Many hide the facts and truth
And let the judge assume
But truth and fact always wins
Your judgment is too soon

There are reasons you knew nothing
Being for your own good
But your judgment sits and vilifies
One's silence misunderstood

In casting out your ignorance
On those you judge below
Your indifference to the truth and fact
More seeds of pain you sow

From the outside looking in
And the inside looking out
The same images projected
But both perceptions were in doubt

What was the outside seeing
When opinion you did throw
Inside viewing was obscured
Some things you needn't know

But only time and distance
Allows one time to grow
A battle with all demons
One will never let it show

No truer is the saying
The truth shall set you free
And only time and distance
Will I find me

On being judged and vilified
You know not what occurred
Your uninformed opinions
From stories that you heard

Now you have my knowledge
Shall I now judge you?
My truth and fact now public
Of the things you never knew!

To my Grandmother

The bravest person I will ever know.

NOTES FOR YOUR CONSIDERATION:

We are being intentionally divided.
Being divided means we are easier to control.
I know this from experience.

Pitching culture against culture, race against race, ethnicity against ethnicity, gender against gender, religion against religion, vaccinated against unvaccinated; health status judgments, income judgments, belief judgments and pitching accepting believers against critical thinkers.

Stop and think before you form an opinion:
Don't cast judgment without full facts:
Acknowledge that sometimes just accepting can be misplaced.
Like I said, I should know.

Realise that you don't know what tomorrow brings, anything can happen to anyone at any time, even to you.

Discrimination and judgmental opinions serve no good purpose.
So stop posting them on your social media accounts for the benefit of the panopticon.

Inform yourself: Look at the road ahead.

LIVE YOUR LIFE ON PURPOSE WHILE YOU CAN

LEFT BLANK FOR THE FOLKS OF THIS TOWN:
LOCATIONS:

LEFT BLANK FOR THE FOLKS OF THIS TOWN:
LOCATIONS:

GOODBYE 1 NARCISSIST ROAD.

Printed in Great Britain
by Amazon

83396798R00120